A
MURDER
REDEEMED

STAR OF JUSTICE SERIES

A
MURDER
REDEEMED

STAR OF JUSTICE SERIES

BRUCE HAMMACK

CHAPTER ONE

"Honey, how much trouble will I be in if I shoot one of my officers?" asked CJ.

David lowered his evening cup of coffee. "Are you planning to kill or wound? Either way, I'm not keen on visiting you in prison."

The porch swing creaked as they scanned the land between their new home and the lazy flowing river a quarter mile down an embankment. The evening sky blazed in assorted shades of orange. Deer foraged under pecan trees on the far side of the ribbon of water as shadows stretched longer with each fleeting minute.

"Let me guess," said David. "Chip Sloan hasn't come to grips with you being the Assistant Chief of Police."

CJ hooked a wandering lock of hair behind her ear. "Is it the fate of every supervisor to have an employee that pushes boundaries?"

"More or less." David raised binoculars. He focused in the direction of the deer but kept talking. "What's he done now?"

She gazed at the sky hoping the Lord had written the

answers to her problems in the stars. He hadn't, so she answered David's question.

"There's an arrogance about Sloan that makes me want to slap him. He's one of those guys who pushes right to the edge, then backs off. He has a particular knack for finding loopholes in policies and procedures. When he finds one, he exploits it and dares you to do something."

"It's obvious he's still holding a grudge against you. How long has it been since your report cost him his job with Waco P.D.?"

"Nine years. All we did was tell the truth."

David kept the binoculars to his eyes. "Then that's the answer to how you handle him. Keep telling the truth. He'll either dig a hole so deep he can't get out, or he'll quit."

The quiet of the evening gave way to the nighttime serenade of cicadas. CJ considered what David said, but found it lacking. "You make it sound so simple. The rules at Agape Christian University aren't the same as they are for state troopers."

"You're missing the point. Some people call it karma. Others use the expression, what goes around comes around. The Bible speaks of it as sowing and reaping. Whatever you want to call it, there's a payday. One instructor at the Highway Patrol Academy explained drunk drivers like this: 'They can definitely get away with drinking and driving, but they won't get away indefinitely. Before you get too lenient, consider how many times that drunk driver didn't get caught.'"

"I hope you're not saying I should ignore Sloan's disrespectful attitude."

David's left hand massaged her neck. She moaned.

"Be strategic. Document everything serious enough to deserve a verbal reprimand, but don't treat Sloan any different from your other officers. He's trying to lay a trap for you. Don't play his game or make it easy on him."

CJ rolled her head as David continued to knead tense muscles. He found a muscle that required particular attention and dug in.

"Right there," said CJ. "That's my Chip Sloan spot. Keep at it until you get him out of there."

"Any other spots?" asked David in a seductive tone. He leaned in to place a light kiss on her neck.

"There might be." CJ paused and reached her left hand over her right shoulder. "Right there."

David sighed. "Not exactly what I meant."

"I know what you meant." She issued a wink. "It's still early. Tell me about your day. Which ranger were you working with?"

"I was on my own. Captain Crow has me compiling data and doing statistical analysis on car thefts in Central Texas. There's been a big uptick, and it doesn't fit the usual pattern. Hardly any recovered vehicles. That means these aren't being taken on joy rides."

CJ rolled her head as David continued working on her neck. "Did you count the four cars we've had stolen from campus this semester?"

"Uh-huh."

"President Cummings is catching heat from the board of regents."

David's lips replaced his hand on her neck.

CJ rose from the swing, stretched and asked, "Are you coming to bed soon?"

David glanced toward the barn. "I need to check on Dad. He didn't seem right at supper tonight."

"I noticed. We were told to expect this. He's only been out of prison a month and the excitement's worn off. Bea said it may take months for him to adjust."

David leaned forward and heaved himself up to his full six foot, three inches. "I'm worried. I need to find something that will give him purpose, or at least something to do."

"Time, honey. Give him time," said CJ.

"I know, but he needs something productive to do now."

"What?"

David's shoulders rose and dropped.

CJ wrapped both arms around her husband and pressed in tight. "Give me a kiss. I'll pray for your dad while I'm washing my face and brushing my teeth."

The kiss rated four on a ten-point scale. Not bad, but far from David's usual effort. He turned as soon as they separated and headed toward a splash of light outside the barn's door.

A worried thirty-year-old woman stared back at CJ as she reached for a towel to dry her face. She mumbled. "Three problems to solve. One: What to do with an employee who hates me. Two: What can I do to help David's dad? And three: Cars being snatched from campus and I don't have a clue who's doing it."

CHAPTER TWO

David's approach to the barn didn't go unnoticed. Sandy, a German shepherd mix, greeted him with tail at full wag. He raked her ribs with his fingertips. "Are you keeping Dad company tonight?"

Light spilled from the twin sliding doors, revealing Bob Harper sitting in a lawn chair with a laptop balanced on his knees. He looked up, grunted an acknowledgement of David's presence, and refocused on the screen.

"What cha' lookin' at, Dad?"

"Surfin' the net."

David dragged a second lawn chair from a stack and settled within talking distance of his father.

In due course, Bob closed the screen and set the computer on a short table by his side. "What's on your mind, son?"

"I wanted to check on you. Are you sure you want to live in the fifth wheel?"

"I'm sure."

"You were quiet at supper. Is something wrong?"

Bob rose to his feet, took a couple of steps into the night

and stuffed his hands into the pockets of his jeans. His staring into darkness didn't last long.

"I'm frustrated with the pace of things. It took less than three months for them to arrest me, try me and send me to prison. The men responsible for killing your mother won't go to trial until summer of next year. It's not right."

"They arrested you over sixteen years ago, and you had a court-appointed attorney who thought a legal brief was a lawyer's underwear." David's attempt at humor earned him an icy stare. "Sorry. I know you want those people to pay, but we have to let the wheels of justice grind away."

"It's a lousy system." He pointed to the laptop. "I've been researching. You won't believe the number of unsolved murder cases there are. Forty percent is one guess, but that's for cases cleared. That's a catch-all term that doesn't necessarily mean anyone was ever convicted." A firm exhalation of breath expressed his disgust. "How can you do your job knowing so many criminals you arrest will never be punished?"

David stared into the night. "I catch 'em and do it by the book. What happens after that is someone else's responsibility."

Bob pointed a finger at him. "It's a lousy system, and it's not the only one."

David leaned back in his chair. He'd been warned to expect this kind of catharsis, and how to react when it came. His job was to listen and let his dad spew it all out.

"What else is rotten?"

His father moved closer, hands on bent knees, and whispered, "How about $1.28 million owed me by the State of Texas for false imprisonment?"

"It's coming, Dad."

He straightened and threw up his hands. "Yeah, sure. I know. The check's in the mail."

"It's coming," said David, his patience wearing thin. "Besides, I gave you a credit card and a debit card. You can buy anything you want, any time you want."

"They took everything I owned in a matter of hours. Why can't some bureaucrat in Austin type in a few keystrokes and pay me what's owed?"

David ran a hand across his face. "I'll call a lawyer tomorrow."

His father's shoulders slumped and his tone softened. "You don't get it, son. I don't want you to do my bidding for me. I need to be independent and pay my own way. It's like I'm still in prison as long as I'm mooching off you and CJ. I'm eating your food, living in your travel trailer in your barn, driving your vehicles and using your credit and debit cards to buy everything else."

"You could move back in the house." David regretted the words as soon as they left his mouth.

The look his father gave him reminded him of similar pursed-lip looks he'd received in high school. "Use your head for more than a place to hang sunglasses. You married less than a year ago. The one thing you two don't need is me under your roof." His father waved a hand in the direction of the door. "I'm not fit company tonight. Go spend time with your wife and don't worry about me. I'll be fine."

They gave an obligatory hug, and David trudged past the swimming pool and up the steps to the back porch. He found CJ already in bed, propped up on pillows.

"How's Dad?" she asked.

"Spewing." He nudged her over and sat on her side of the bed. A detailed account of the conversation followed.

"That doesn't sound like your father." She patted the space where David slept. "Want to talk about it some more?"

He rose. "I'm talked out. Don't you have a quick fix for what's ailing him?"

"I'll talk to Bea tomorrow and see what she recommends."

David massaged his temples. "Caring for a parent isn't easy."

"Pray more worry less." She grabbed his hand and pulled. "Give me a goodnight kiss, and make it better than the last one."

AN OFFENSIVE NOISE JERKED CJ OUT OF SLEEP. SHE glanced at the bedside clock that read eleven-fifty. A book of Dashiell Hammett short stories fell to the floor as she reached for her phone.

"Who is it?" asked David.

"Sgt. Ramirez. This won't be a social call." She cleared her throat. "What's up, Sergeant?"

An accented voice responded. "Another stolen car. Broken glass on the parking lot of Mays Hall."

"Is the owner sure?"

"One hundred percent. He made a pizza run three hours ago and parked it in a dark corner. He discovered it missing about forty minutes ago."

"Why was he leaving the dorm so late... or early, whatever it is?"

"Problems with his señorita. She lives on the other side of campus and he didn't want to walk."

"Do you need me to come in?"

"Not unless you want to supervise taking pictures of broken glass and an empty parking space."

"No thanks. Were you the responding officer?"

"Sloan took the call from dispatch. I was in town taking a coffee break." He paused. "I thought you should know since this is number four."

"Five," said CJ.

"Oh, yeah." He paused. "Should I call Chief Sylvester?"

"Have the city and county been notified?"

"Sloan made sure of it as soon as he got the vehicle description and license number from the student."

CJ made a poor attempt to stifle a yawn. "No need to wake the Chief. Make sure you double-check everywhere on campus."

"We're already on it."

CJ thought for a couple of seconds. "Tell Sloan he did a good job." It occurred to her that Chip Sloan would likely file a grievance if he didn't get a commendation. He'd done his job and deserved a pat on the back. Nothing more.

CJ looked again at the clock. "Tell the officers on duty I'll be in early for a mandatory meeting."

CHAPTER THREE

CJ wheeled her university-issued Chevy Tahoe into a reserved parking space in front of a sad excuse for a building. A converted Korean War army barracks, it sat on the back side of the sprawling campus of Agape Christian University. Its location, across the street from the Ag Barn, complete with all the smells and sounds of livestock, added additional ambiance to the Police Department. The building's non-academic function accounted for it being the last thing considered on annual budgets for twenty-nine of the last thirty years.

She continued to stare at the building, allowing her thoughts concerning the police department to run free. Things changed last year when John Sylvester took over as Chief of Police. Despite his youthful appearance, he wrangled the board of regents into action by prioritizing a new building for the police department. His timing couldn't have been better. All major construction projects on campus were complete, enrollment hit the desired capacity and alumni fundraisers were reaping excellent results.

For now, however, CJ looked at the asbestos-shingle siding

and moaned. She made a last check of her face in the mirror and headed for the front door, timing it so she'd be there when third shift, 10:00 p.m. to 6:00 a.m., ended. Normally they'd turn in any paperwork and head home. Not today.

The inside of the building qualified as an eyesore. Short pile carpet unraveled at the seams and the floor groaned under the weight of anyone larger than a child. She couldn't remember the last time all the florescent lights burned without at least one blinking like it had a nervous twitch.

"Good morning," she announced as she stepped through the door of a room that smelled of strong coffee. The gathering place had various names: squad room, muster room, shift-change room, or the officers' doughnut and coffee room. No matter the name, it served its function, but didn't evoke pride.

She hadn't made it to the podium before a voice spoke above the rest. "Are we being credited with overtime?"

Chip Sloan slouched in a chair with his legs fully extended and crossed at the ankles. Jet-black hair, slicked straight back with enough hair product to last a normal man three days, glistened under the fluorescent lights.

CJ counted to three and didn't respond to the question. "I wanted you all to stay a few minutes this morning so I could hear what you have to say about the latest stolen car. I also want to hear any ideas you might have for ways of stopping these thefts."

"You didn't answer my question," said Sloan. "If you're paying us, I'll stay. If not, I have better things to do."

CJ counted to five. "I called Chief Sylvester on my way here and he approved thirty minutes overtime."

CJ issued a wide, phony smile. "Officer Sloan, I understand you were the first officer to respond. Start when you received the call and give us details on how you handled the report of another stolen car."

"It's in my report."

"I realize that, but we all might benefit from a first-hand extemporaneous account."

Sloan opened a folder, took out a two-page report of the incident and read it word-for-word.

"Thank you, Officer Sloan," said CJ.

She shifted her gaze to Sgt. Ramirez. "Sergeant, would you relate what actions you took?"

The sergeant picked up where Sloan left off. He gave a brief, factual report that concluded with, "It looked like a smash and grab. The same as the others."

CJ waved a hand at the gathering of four other officers. "I'd like to get input from everyone. Give me your theories of who could steal these cars. Even if it sounds improbable or crazy, write it down and turn it in to me before you leave."

"What a waste of time," mumbled Sloan.

"Next," said CJ above Sloan's complaint, "I want you to write any suggestions of what we might do to bring these thefts to an end. All of you are outstanding officers. You see things at night other shifts miss. I'm open to any suggestions."

"You might try getting a real-live detective who knows how to investigate," said Sloan.

"Sloan—"

He sprang to his feet and pointed at her. "Officer Sloan or Mr. Sloan. That's how the policies manual says you're to address me."

"Sloan," said CJ with steel in her voice. "You went before an impartial promotion board. Detective Vasquez is the detective and you're not. Get over it. The attitude you're displaying should tell you one of the reasons you didn't get the job." She paused. "Go home. You have nothing constructive to add."

He shot her a look of total defiance.

"Out! Now!"

He issued an oily smile. "Glad to. I'll just pick up a grievance form on my way out."

"Get several. You'll need them."

JOHN SYLVESTER ARRIVED WITH A SPRING IN HIS STEP AND a tube of blueprints tucked under his arm. He looked like a kid with an unopened Christmas present.

"Here they are," he crowed.

CJ followed him to his office, the only room in the building to receive a facelift in the last ten years. She intended to tell him about her run-in with Sloan and wanted to go over the latest stolen car. His priorities lay elsewhere.

"At last," he said. "The architects took forever. I want you to go over these after I do. If we need changes, now is the time to make them. Once they're approved, we'll have to live with it."

CJ regarded her boss. He wasn't usually so animated. In fact, it was normal for him to have his head buried in spreadsheets or fixed on his computer. From shoes to the top of his dark hair, he measured five foot, six inches. Wire-framed glasses did little to hide a pleasant, suntanned face. Running marathons kept away any hint of a bulge around his midsection, a condition that afflicted many cops in their early to mid-thirties.

He emptied the cardboard tube of its contents and spread them out on a wooden conference table. He anchored the corners of the blueprints with a tape dispenser, scissors, a trophy and an empty coffee mug. Only then did he look up.

"Tell me about the stolen car."

"Another smash and grab," said CJ. She waited for a reaction.

He abandoned the table, circled his desk and eased himself into a black executive chair. He looked at a spot somewhere on the wall over her shoulder. "That makes five this semester." His focus shifted back to CJ.

"Did you come in to investigate?"

She shook her head. "Sergeant Ramirez called me a little before midnight. Officer Sloan responded to the call and did everything required. The city and county were notified and given the license and description of the vehicle. The two of them took witness statements from everyone that might have seen anything, and the third shift officers made a thorough search of the campus parking lots and anywhere else they could think of. Some shards of broken glass and an empty parking spot at Mays Hall were the only evidence to document."

John rested his right elbow on his desk and cupped his chin in his palm. His eyes darted back and forth and his brow wrinkled. "Cameras caught nothing?"

CJ shook her head. "Just like the other times, the student parked the car in a blind spot of the parking lot. A driver with visor down and wearing a mask dropped off someone who wore a hoody and kept his back to the camera. The car carrying the thieves had stolen plates."

John looked at his Apple watch. "I have classes to teach this morning. What are your plans?"

"As soon as Maria arrives, I'll fill her in and we'll go to Mays Hall. We'll stand where the student parked his car and look to see if any dorm window might have had a view. It's a long shot, but we might get lucky."

"Tell me about the car," said John.

"A fifteen-year-old Mustang. Custom rims and all kinds of after-market gadgets."

John nodded. "Was entry gained through the passenger side?"

CJ dipped her chin and returned it. "Smash the glass, unlock the doors, go to the driver's seat, pop the ignition and they're gone in less than a minute."

John glanced at the table. His look told her he'd rather be looking at blueprints than concentrating on stolen cars.

A deep intake of air preceded CJ's next words. "There's two other things."

John shifted his gaze to meet hers.

"David is working on a statistical analysis of stolen cars all over central Texas. ACU isn't the only place that's reporting a rash of stolen cars and trucks."

The chair squeaked as John sat up straighter. "Now that's interesting. Up to now, I've assumed these thefts were our problem alone. This speaks to something much bigger and well organized."

He rose from his chair. "I need to get to class. What was the second thing?"

CJ didn't want to burden him, but he needed to know what happened at shift change. "I had a run-in with Officer Sloan this morning. He pushed my buttons until I sort of lost it on him and kicked him out of the room. He took a stack of grievance forms with him when he left."

John groaned. "He's been a pain since he didn't get that promotion." He took a step toward the door and stopped. "We have more important things on our plates than worrying about what a disgruntled employee might or might not do. We'll handle the grievance if he files it."

A sly smile lifted the corners of John's mouth. "You might like to know I've been receiving phone calls from other departments. Sloan's been making inquiries, and he's put in an application at the city. He may not be our problem much longer."

A grin crossed CJ's face. She followed John into the hall. "Why don't you and Dotty and the girls come out to the house tonight? Bea and Billie Paul are coming over for barbeque. You could pick David's brain. He should be pretty far along with his analysis by this evening."

"I'll call Dotty on my way to class and make sure our schedule is clear. I'll let you know later." He turned and strode to the door carrying a forensic accounting textbook.

The front door rattled shut and the dispatcher hollered through the hole in her glass window.

"CJ, President Cummings wants to see you in her office."

"How did she sound?"

"Impatient."

CJ mumbled, "It's one of those days."

CHAPTER FOUR

Snarled traffic and the distance back to the police department made CJ's decision to hoof it across campus an easy one. Besides, the ten-minute walk would help clear her mind of the run-in with Chip Sloan and give her a chance to think of what she might say to Alice Cummings.

After scaling the exterior steps of the Administration Building, CJ ascended two flights of stairs and slipped into the ladies' restroom where she checked her hair and makeup. She squatted to see the top of her head in the mirror. Being six feet tall had its disadvantages.

The floor leading to the president's office gleamed so brightly it would earn a nod of approval, even from a prickly drill sergeant. She pushed open the last door on the left and received an emotionless nod from the president's secretary.

"Go on in, CJ. She's expecting you."

The inner sanctum commanded an exceptional view of the campus. Academic buildings, some looking wise with age, and some rising like giant brick boxes, climbed above the tops of live oak trees that had to be saplings when the state came into existence. Sidewalks spider-webbed their way through manicured lawns, hedges and crepe myrtles.

The office itself mirrored its occupant, stately and refined, but without a hint of ostentation. Alice Cummings had the ability to maintain good posture, whether standing or sitting. CJ's mother would describe her as having bearing. But why? Was it her collar-length hair that looked like spun silver and hung perfectly? Perhaps it was her choice of outfits, business suits that fit like they were hand-tailored. Could it be the way she spoke with crisp diction and maintained near-constant eye contact? Whatever it was, Alice Cummings could charm with a smile, or devastate with a glare, as the occasion dictated.

CJ looked for clues of the president's mood as she spoke on the phone and pointed for CJ to take a seat in a chair in front of her desk. Nothing stood out.

"Yes, Charley, I have it on my calendar. How could I forget? Your barbecue for university presidents is the highlight of my year. Thanks for the call. I'll see you in November."

After manipulating her cell phone, Alice placed it on her desk and folded her hands in front of her. "I've put it on vibrate." She paused, "What is it about politicians? They stay in campaign mode every day of their lives."

"By Charley, I'm assuming you were speaking with our governor?"

Alice nodded. "He's a dear old cuss, but he can be intense." She looked at CJ with piercing blue eyes. "I guess you know all about that, don't you?"

"Governor Wainwright had me agreeing to be a Texas Ranger before I knew what hit me. It took a full week before I came to my senses and turned down the job."

"His loss is our gain," said Alice. "And speaking of losses. I understand we have another stolen car."

"Last night from the parking lot at Mays Hall."

"Tell me about it."

CJ took in a deep breath and relayed the facts from the time she received the late-night phone call until she spoke with John Sylvester. Alice didn't move throughout the narrative.

Despite her ability to not over-react to disquieting news, the information caused a scowl to cross Alice's face. "This is much worse than I thought. I never dreamed these thefts could be part of organized criminal activity. Are you sure? I don't want to cry wolf to the board of regents."

"Car thefts are up all over Central Texas. It's serious enough that the Rangers have taken David off all other cases."

"What can we do to stop these thefts?"

"There's a long list of things. To name a few, we could substantially increase lighting on campus, beef up police presence and install a much more comprehensive system of surveillance cameras."

"You're talking about long-term solutions that aren't in the current budget." Alice cast her gaze out a window. "John and I were hard-pressed to get the new building for the police department approved. I see choppy water if we go back to the regents with our hands out for additional money. Any other ideas?"

"John and Dotty are coming over for barbeque chicken tonight. Join us. David, Billy Paul and Bea will be there, too. We can brainstorm things that won't wreck the budget."

Alice stood and circled her desk, giving CJ her cue to leave.

"What time?"

"Six thirty, and bring nothing but an appetite."

Alice stopped before they reached the door. "How's your father-in-law adjusting?"

"He's bored. Every tool, nut, bolt and washer in the barn is in its place and labeled. I guess it's his mechanical engineer mind that wants to have a place for everything and everything in its place."

A glimmer in her eye accompanied a hint of a smile. "I look forward to meeting him."

CHAPTER FIVE

"Must have coffee," mumbled CJ as she meandered her way across campus. The student union building with its gourmet coffee shop might as well have been a homing beacon. She picked up her stride. Cutting between cars, she crossed the street and entered the hub of student life on campus. Taking a hard left, she entered The College Grind, a hive of noise, laughter, shots and double shots of caffeine and moan-inducing pastries. After gaining four pounds in two weeks, CJ had to impose a one-per-week limit, and that only applied if she ran two miles that morning. She'd skipped her dawn run to come to work early. No matter how loud the scones, eclairs, cinnamon rolls and apple fritters called her name, she'd abstain from pastries and stick with a tall coffee.

Three baristas struggled to keep up with demand as CJ stared into the glass case. Only the call of "Next!" saved her from temptation's sticky hand.

Looking around, CJ noticed something amiss. "Where's Yari?" she asked the barista.

"Called in sick," said a girl with lavender hair and a pierced eyebrow.

With temptation pushed back, CJ ordered coffee. Waiting, she scanned the room to pick up on the vibe of the students. Mid-term exams drew near, so the mood was not as leisurely as the previous week. Many students ordered their supercharged drinks to go and left for classes or to find quiet places to study.

CJ saw the upraised arm of a woman waving with abandon. A smile crept across CJ's face. She retrieved her coffee and wove her way through a sea of tables, chairs and youthful bodies.

"Get yourself over here and sit down," implored the woman with bright red lipstick and big, blonde, southern hair.

Obeying the regal command, CJ sat and patted Bea Stargate on her arm. "The bees are buzzing this morning."

Bea introduced each of the three girls at the table she presided over then said, "You three honey bees run along. Assistant Chief Harper and I have business to discuss."

The three gave their mentor a hug and chirped their way out of The College Grind.

Bea cast her gaze around the room and exclaimed, "Isn't this the best place in the world? I can almost taste the excitement and dreams of these young men and women."

Bea cast her gaze at CJ. Her countenance cleared and her voice lowered. "I heard about the stolen car. You didn't get much sleep last night, did you?"

"I got the call before midnight and came in early this morning. I've already had an unpleasant encounter with one of my officers and Alice called me into her office."

Bea glanced up at the clock on the wall. "It's not even nine o'clock yet."

"Yeah. I hope it gets better."

A comforting hand came forward and rested on CJ's hand. "Frettin' never helps. You'll catch whoever's doing this."

"Speaking of," said CJ. "I've invited a few others to join us for supper. But I'm afraid it's going to be a time to talk shop. David told me last night that car thefts are up all over Central Texas. I invited Alice, John and Dotty to see if maybe we could all come up with some solutions."

"Lord have mercy," whispered Bea. "Billy Paul told me last night one of his excavator operators had his pickup truck stolen. It was older, but in perfect shape."

"That fits the M.O."

CJ didn't have a chance to say anything else. A rangy student wearing faded jeans and a purple t-shirt stood in front of her. Bushy eyebrows draped over tired eyes.

"Are you Assistant Chief Harper?" he asked.

CJ nodded.

"Why aren't you looking for my car instead of sitting in here drinking coffee?"

In a calm voice CJ asked, "Are you Braden Lockwood?"

"Yeah."

"Please have a seat and we'll talk."

"Talk? Is that all you cops know how to do?"

CJ stood. "I know you're upset. Please sit down. I'll tell you everything that's being done to retrieve your car."

His brown hair shook from side to side. "It's too late, and you know it. My car had a book value of seven grand, but I'd put that much more into it. The custom rims and tires alone are worth four grand." He looked away and then brought a smoldering gaze to bear. "I'm no fool. My car is already in pieces. Can't you people do a better job of protecting our property?"

He spun on the heel of his Converse tennis shoes and headed for the door.

CJ looked at Bea. "It's definitely one of those days." She paused. "I guess I should say two days and not just one."

Bea's raised eyebrows bid CJ to continue.

Pushing her cup of coffee to the middle of the table, CJ leaned on her elbows. "My father-in-law isn't adjusting like we expected. David had a rather unpleasant talk with him last night."

"Oh?"

"It seems Bob resents what we're doing for him. David said he used the word 'mooching.'"

Bea nodded. "You need a temporary money solution." Her countenance brightened. "I've got it. Call your banker and ask him to extend Bob a line of credit. Make sure he knows you'll back any purchases until Bob's check comes in."

"Will they do that?"

Bea's smile broadened. "They won't pass up a million-dollar deposit, or risk making you and David mad."

"Thanks, Bea. That's the perfect solution, at least for his money problems. But that's not all that's going on with Bob—he's bored out of his mind. Sandy's a great dog, but she's not much on conversation."

"Bored. That sounds right for his situation, and it's not a bad thing. He's itching to find something to give him purpose. With money to spend, he'll soon figure out what to do with himself."

"I'm not so sure."

Before Bea could offer one of her patented pep talks, CJ's phone came to life. She examined the screen and enabled the call. "Maria, what's up?"

"You need to come to Mays Hall. I've found something interesting."

CHAPTER SIX

Mays Hall sat three-quarters of a mile from the Student Union Building. CJ calculated the time it would take her to return to the police department for her vehicle and opted to walk. The brisk air in her face invigorated her and the distance gave her time to think. It also gave her an opportunity to hope what Detective Maria Vasquez found was something of value. She set a brisk pace and arrived winded.

A remote spot under a canopy of tree limbs offered scant hope someone had witnessed the theft. Maria rose from a crouch. She held out an open palm covered in a blue latex glove.

"Look," said Maria. She stood next to a vacant parking spot. Shards of glass lay at her feet and a larger piece in her hand.

CJ looked at the proffered glass. This wasn't the big break she'd hoped for. "We already know about the broken glass. They must have broken out the passenger side window to gain entrance. It's the same M.O. as the other thefts."

Maria lifted her palm. "Take a closer look at the glass."

"Lend me your other glove." CJ threaded it on and picked up the shard.

"Look at it in the sun," said Maria.

CJ's raised the shard into sunlight. "This glass is brown."

Maria nodded and smiled. "Not clear or tinted blue or dark gray."

"Holy smokes," said CJ. Her mind went into overdrive. "That means either the glass was already here, or all the glass fell into the car."

"Highly unlikely," said Maria.

CJ thought harder. "Or someone planted the glass to make it look like they broke out the passenger side window."

"If that's the case, how did they get in?"

CJ stared at the blank parking spot. "Coat hanger, lock-jock, pried the window open enough to push the door unlock button with something long and thin."

Maria shook her head. "Possible, but I don't think so. This looks staged. It's confined to a small area."

"There's another possibility. Whoever took the car had a key." CJ turned and stepped toward Maria's car. "Let's get back to the office. If I'm right, you need to find the car's owner. Let's see if he still has his keys or if his girlfriend might have a set that's gone missing."

THE GROWL COMING FROM CJ'S STOMACH TOLD HER THE breakfast of low-fat yogurt and a piece of whole-wheat toast wasn't sufficient to last until noon. Footsteps and voices approached her door. The male's voice sounded familiar and distraught.

CJ rose and met Maria and Braden as they appeared in her doorway. "I'm sorry to interrupt your day, Mr. Lockwood.

Has Detective Vasquez explained why we needed you to come in?"

He shrugged. "Not really."

"Have a seat. We came across something interesting this morning that we think you can help us with."

Three chairs formed a triangle in front of CJ's desk. Braden slouched in his chair and swung his right tennis shoe over his left knee. Maria took her place beside him while CJ retrieved the largest piece of glass found in the parking lot.

CJ held the glass between Braden's eyes and the florescent ceiling light. "We found this on the ground beside your car, along with similar pieces of glass. Was your passenger window this color?"

His response came with speed. "Who tints their windows brown? My car had after-market tinting. You know, the kind that goes on in a dark sheet and sets with a heat gun. I had mine done professionally."

"That's the conclusion we reached," said CJ. "This means the glass found beside your car came from somewhere else. Did you notice it on the ground when you pulled into the parking spot?"

His mop of hair shook. "I'm careful where I park. I think I would have noticed broken glass."

Braden looked away and heaved a breath. Was he hiding something or grieving the loss of his prize possession? Perhaps he just didn't like the police.

Whatever the reason for his apparent disdain, CJ pressed on. "We've come up with several explanations for there being no glass from your car's window on the ground. Does anyone but you have a set of keys?"

He straightened his posture. "My parents live in Tyler. That's the only other set."

"Did you have a spare key hidden somewhere on the exterior of your car?"

"I thought about getting one of those magnetic key holders, but I never got around to it. I always keep my keys in my pocket so it never seemed to be a priority." He reached into the left front pocket of his jeans and withdrew a ring with six or seven keys. "This is the only key."

CJ acknowledged the key with a tight smile. "What about your girlfriend? Does she have a key?"

"Are you accusing Candice of stealing my car?"

CJ held up her palms to block the rebuke. "Not at all. We're trying to find your car and put an end to the car thefts." She leaned forward and lowered her voice. "It's my job to ask questions. Most of them don't lead us anywhere, or they take us down dead-end streets. The question I asked is legitimate. You had a fight with your girlfriend then your car went missing. It's not much of a leap to think she might have taken your car in anger. I've seen students pull dumb stunts when they're mad."

The rebuke carried enough authority to cause Braden to sit up straight. "Candice couldn't have taken it. She had a cold and didn't leave her dorm last night."

CJ cast her gaze to Maria. The unspoken look was Maria's signal to follow up and make sure Braden's alibi for his girlfriend was legitimate.

CJ pressed on. "Could anyone in your dorm have gotten your keys? What about your roommate?"

Braden issued a response that led to another dead end. "My roommate backed out at the last minute and never started classes. I keep the door locked when I'm not there. Besides, my keys stay in my pocket."

"Do other students come into your room?"

"Never," he said with finality. "I partied hard last year and my grades showed it. My parents cut off my allowance and gave me one more chance to pull up my GPA. I'm taking eighteen hours and I work at night until ten-thirty. Outside of school and work, I spend my time studying and with Candice."

The well of information had run dry. CJ stood, a non-verbal clue the interview had concluded. To formalize it, she said, "Thank you for your time, Braden. We'll be in contact if we have any updates."

"Did anything we talked about today do any good? I mean, what about my car? What are the chances I'll ever see it again?"

CJ put her hand on his shoulder and looked him in the eye. "You're asking two questions. You want to know if we'll ever find your car. It's been missing at least twelve hours. Every cop in Central Texas is on the lookout for it. There's still a possibility someone will spot it." She paused. "Because of all the after-market additions you made to the car, I'd say your chances of getting it back intact are approaching zero. I believe the person, or persons, who took it targeted it. They knew the value was in all the expensive additions and parts."

Braden hung his head. "Even if you found her, she'd never be the same. I guess it's time for my folks to call the insurance company and get what they can. At least it'll be something." He paused. "You said I was asking two questions. What was the second?"

"Was this interview a waste of time? You didn't use those words, but we know that's what you were thinking."

He nodded.

"Investigations are like building a house with ninety-five percent of the materials shoddy and unusable. We will discard most facts. Some will lay the foundation. Others will build the walls. Eventually, we'll put together enough to catch these guys. Because you cooperated, we now have more information than we did. I can't help but think what you told us will eventually help us."

Maria piped up. "Come on, Braden. I'll give you a ride to wherever you want to go."

"The library. I have a calculus test tomorrow."

CJ saw Braden and Maria to her office door and closed it behind them. She returned to her desk, picked up her landline phone and dialed. A chipper female voice answered. "First National Bank of Riverview. How may I direct your call?"

"This is CJ Harper. I'd like to speak to Mr. Hewitt."

After the usual delay when someone asks for the bank's president, a booming voice came on the line. "CJ. Good to hear from you. How can I help?"

"I need you to do a favor for me. You'll make a little money on it and get a new customer that will deposit over a million dollars."

"You have my attention. Keep talking."

CHAPTER SEVEN

A cloud of mesquite smoke enveloped Billy Paul Stargate as he stood in front of a combination barbecue pit and smoker. A ring of premature silver hair peeked out from under a green John Deere baseball cap. His standard chilly weather uniform of flannel shirt, bib overalls and scuffed work boots completed his ensemble. He slathered on a topcoat of his secret sauce and turned the chicken halves. "Twenty more minutes and these yard birds will be ready to put on a plate."

Bob stood in Billy Paul's shadow, watching every move as if the chickens might resurrect and take flight at any moment.

CJ claimed her favorite seat, the porch swing overlooking the river of her and David's three-hundred-acre farm. She also had a view of the swimming pool, the barn, and the barbecue pit that occupied the attention of two of the men in attendance. Once again, she noticed how much David looked like a younger version of his father, minus the gray hair.

Two vehicles approached and parked on the new concrete driveway. John and Dotty Sylvester piled out of their vehicle.

John had not changed out of his dress slacks and sports coat, but as a nod to the informality of the setting, he'd left his tie behind. Dotty, all five-foot-two inches of her, wore jeans, a denim shirt and hiking boots.

"Where are the girls?" asked Bea from her seat next to CJ.

The newlywed couple walked hand-in-hand across the backyard and settled in patio chairs on the porch. Dotty said, "We dropped them off at a friend's birthday party. I can't imagine what a house full of twelve-year-old girls sound like when they get full of cake and sugary drinks. I'll take the quiet of your back porch any day."

John agreed with "Amen to that."

CJ smiled at her boss' comment, but noticed he had sweat on his upper lip. He hadn't had time to exercise before coming over and the weather wasn't warm enough today to make anyone sweat.

CJ's attention was diverted from John when she heard a car door slam. "Oh, good. Alice is here. I wasn't sure she would come."

Alice dressed down for the occasion, which meant she wore wool slacks, a cashmere sweater and a tailored black jacket. As always, she looked like she'd stepped out of the window of a high-end boutique.

Instead of joining the women and John on the porch, Alice walked toward David's father and Billy Paul at the large steel cooker. CJ saw Billy Paul introduce Bob and Alice. After a few minutes, CJ noticed the two of them move away from Billy Paul, upwind from the smoke. Judging from Alice's smile, it looked like they were getting along pretty well.

Never at a loss for words, Dotty regaled CJ and Bea with tales of her and John's daughters and how they were adjusting to being step-sisters. In the brief moments when Dotty let another's words intrude on her narrative, Bea filled the voids with questions.

CJ stole glances at Bob and Alice and wondered what they were talking and laughing about. She wished Dotty and Bea would follow John's lead and look on passively as life ambled by at a leisurely pace. No such luck with those two. When they were together conversation flowed as endlessly as the river. CJ looked up as birds in the nearby trees were startled into flight by Bea's high-pitched laughter. CJ contributed a smile to the conversation. No matter what was going on at work, they had a good life and good friends.

Voices quietened when the lid to the pit clanged shut. Billy Paul announced, "Ten more minutes and we'll be ready to take these yard birds inside."

Alice and Bob joined the group and Bob launched into a tale of how the president of the bank called him. John interrupted, "I'm afraid Dotty and I need to leave. I'm not feeling great. But before we go, we have a serious problem on campus that needs solving." He turned to Alice. "Would you give us an update on what the chairman of the board of regents told you today?"

Alice stood and cleared her throat. "First, let me express my appreciation to David and CJ for inviting me here tonight and for Billy Paul's usual magic at the barbecue pit."

After the affirmations died down, Alice continued. "I received a phone call this afternoon from the chairman of the board of regents. He reported an ever-increasing number of correspondences from interested parties expressing displeasure with the rash of car thefts from campus. Things have not reached critical mass yet, but calls for action are increasing at an alarming rate."

Billy Paul sat up straight. "I haven't checked my emails today. What are they threatening to do?"

CJ considered Billy Paul's question. As a past president of the board of regents, he'd weathered the storms of criticism and kept the university pointed in the right direction. While still on the board, he didn't yield the power he once did.

Alice looked at Billy Paul, but the volume of her words meant they were for everyone in attendance. "As you know, we replaced several members of the board of regents this past spring. To be frank, I used up a lot of political goodwill in cajoling the regents into approving a new building for the police department."

Dotty couldn't keep quiet. "But that old building is a fire-trap and an eyesore."

"Granted," said Alice. "But think about the personalities of the people on the board. They're all successful and results-oriented. They come with their own priorities and beliefs on how the university should operate."

David chimed in. "Alice, do these people realize that car thefts have gone through the roof throughout Central Texas in the last four months?"

Alice lifted her chin slightly. "Their focus is on the university. If ACU gets the reputation of being a place that isn't safe for a student's property or person, prospective students and their parents will think twice about making our university their first choice."

Dotty perched on the edge of the chair. "Give it to us straight, Alice. What did you hear today?"

"I won't characterize them as threats, but there are two things some board members are considering. The first is canceling the new building for the police department."

CJ looked at John. His shoulders sagged as sweat formed drops on his forehead.

"And the second?" asked CJ.

"Remember," said Alice. "We have not yet reached the point of crisis. However, the remedy many top executives use when things go wrong is to find someone to blame."

John broke in. "That means me. They'll fire me for incompetence."

Alice didn't correct him.

David stood. "There's a simple solution to this. We work together to catch these guys."

All heads nodded. David said, "After we eat, we'll brainstorm and come up with an action plan."

John stood but fell back in his chair.

Dotty grabbed his hand. "What's wrong?"

He shrugged and gave a weak smile. "I don't know. Sharp pain." His hand covered his lower abdomen. "It's been bad off and on all day."

He tried to stand but fell back again. His head lolled to the side and his eyes rolled upward.

"John!" shouted Dotty.

Voices overrode other voices. David moved to where John sat and scooped him up in his arms.

CJ barked out, "My SUV. David's driving. Dotty, you and John in the back seat. Everyone else come to the hospital when you can. I'll notify them we're coming in hot."

CHAPTER EIGHT

The doctor wore blue scrubs and a surgical mask pulled down around her throat. A cloth cap hid what appeared to be a significant crown of ink-black hair. Her words carried only a slight hint of an accent.

CJ held Dotty's hand as the woman said, "Mrs. Sylvester, your husband suffered a ruptured appendix. The surgery took longer than expected. We found significant infiltration from the appendix into the abdominal cavity. I did my best to clean it out, and I've placed him on a regimen of strong antibiotics."

Fingers dug into CJ's hand. Dotty mumbled but couldn't form questions.

CJ asked, "What's your primary concern, Doctor?"

"Peritonitis. It's an infection of the abdomen's inner wall. It's always a concern with a surgery of this nature."

Dotty found her voice. "When can he come home?"

The doctor let out a deep breath and addressed Dotty, "Your husband's condition is critical. The good news is, he's in excellent physical condition." She paused and allowed herself a brief smile. "He has one of the highest thresholds of pain I've ever seen. From the level of infiltration, I'd say the appendix burst sometime last night or early this morning. It's a good thing he passed out, and you got him here when you did."

Dotty looked down. "When he's focused, he can block out anything. I didn't know that included pain. Can I see him?"

"He's in recovery and then he'll go to ICU. Gown-up and wear a mask before you go in."

CJ looked down on the doctor. "No other visitors?"

"Perhaps I haven't expressed myself as I should have. 'Critical' means close to death."

CJ AND DOTTY RETURNED TO THE WAITING ROOM. DAVID found the remote to the wall-mounted television and turned it off. Everyone from the dinner party waited in silence as CJ settled Dotty in a chair next to Bea.

"John's condition is critical," said CJ.

The gravity of the words descended on the group like a thick curtain. After long seconds, energy seeped back into the room. Alice delivered a box of tissues. Bea held tight to Dotty's hand. "Don't you worry about the home front. Billy Paul picked up Hope and Faith from the birthday party. He has their teeth brushed and they're tucked in bed. I called your mom and dad and told them. They're on their way."

"Are you sure Billy Paul doesn't mind?"

"They're asleep and he's like an old horse. He can sleep standing up if need be."

"Thanks, Bea," said Dotty. "It sounds terrible, but I forgot all about the girls being at the birthday party."

An hour later, David stated he would be of more use reviewing the data on the car thefts and developing strategies. He called a fellow state trooper for a ride home. After he left, Alice announced she'd return David's father to their farm. She also volunteered Bob to help her put up food from the aborted feast. He issued a shallow bow and said, "My pleasure."

A nurses' aide, who didn't look old enough to vote, entered the near-empty waiting room and summoned Dotty to follow her to ICU.

After twenty minutes, it occurred to CJ that Alice didn't have to take David's dad home. He could have gone with David and the highway patrolman. Also, David could put beans, coleslaw, potato salad and leftover chicken in the refrigerator. The more she ran an internal tape of memories from the evening, the more she realized Bob and Alice had talked extensively. In fact, they had been downright chummy toward each other.

A multi-generational family entered the waiting room and ended the relative solitude. The man wearing grimy clothes, plopped himself in a chair and washed a stubbled chin with a calloused hand. The two boys, stair-step versions of each other, sat as far away from the man as they could, which put them within arm's reach of CJ. Their shirtsleeves glistened with discharge from their noses and they coughed without making the slightest effort to cover their mouths.

CJ retreated to the hallway.

It didn't take long before Dotty joined her with brow furrowed and lips pursed thin across her teeth. "They kicked me out."

CJ took her friend by the arm and guided her away. "Let's go to the cafeteria. The children in the waiting room are spreading germs that haven't been named yet."

Three steps into their journey, Dotty broke down. Her

chest heaved, and she cupped her hands over her face. She croaked, "They have him on a ventilator. So many tubes and monitors." She balled a fist and hit her thigh. "It's not fair! I can't lose him. I can't."

"And you won't. He's one of the healthiest men I know, and he needs you to be strong."

Dotty straightened her back, pulled her palms down her face and took one halting step, and then another. Soon, they found themselves in the cafeteria drinking black coffee not more than several hours old.

CJ had known Dotty for nine-plus years, they'd been roommates at the Highway Patrol Academy. How odd to see the bubbly blonde in such a subdued state. She'd always been the picture of confidence and expectation of good days ahead. The reality of the possibility of losing her husband didn't fit in Dotty's well-plotted plans for the future.

After a deep sigh, Dotty reached for her cell phone. Her thumbs flew over the face of the phone and she hit the send icon. "I'm telling Mom and Dad to come here to the cafeteria."

The reply came back almost instantly. Dotty pushed her phone so they both could read it.

On our way.

The clock on the wall of the cafeteria read 2:00 a.m. when CJ excused herself to go home. Dotty's mom would leave in a few minutes to relieve Bea and Billy Paul. Dotty would sit with her father all night in the waiting room, praying for healing and another chance to be at John's bedside if he woke.

A shiver went down CJ's back as she trudged to her car. The October morning had a bite to it; or perhaps it was fatigue setting in after the release of adrenaline wore off.

The journey home required CJ to pass by the ACU

campus. Despite her fatigue, she made a slow drive through campus. Who knows, she might get lucky and happen upon a car being stolen.

CHAPTER NINE

Even a university campus slows down after midnight, especially if mid-term exams are looming. Foot traffic was practically non-existent, but more lights than usual burned in the dorm rooms. Some would stay on all night as students either crammed or fell asleep at their desks.

The SUV eased its way down a street that bordered the west side of the campus. The heater kept her feet and legs toasty, but with the driver and passenger windows rolled down so she could hear better, the cold nibbled at CJ's fingers and cheeks. She turned onto the campus road that divided the police department and the Ag Barn. A turn to her right brought her on a north-south street where Sergeant Ramirez's car sat next to the curb.

Expecting to find him in the patrol car with the heater keeping him toasty, she parked behind him, but noticed his car wasn't running. She moved along the side of his car and placed her hand on the hood. The cold metal told her he must be on foot and had been for quite some time.

She nodded her approval as she returned to her car and lifted the microphone to her radio.

"ACU 02 to 09."

She waited for ten or twelve seconds before she repeated the call.

He responded, "09, go ahead 02."

"What's your 20?"

"On foot. Walking to my car in front of the science building."

Sgt. Ramirez didn't have a reputation for being fleet of foot. He took life at a slow, steady pace. It didn't surprise her when she waited several minutes for him to appear from shadows on the south side of the three-story building.

Before CJ could speak the sergeant asked, "How's Chief Sylvester?"

"Not good. Does everyone know?"

"We heard about it in shift change. Second shift officers picked up your radio traffic. They said you and your husband passed the campus doing at least eighty. Lieutenant Grimes called the hospital and verified it was the chief."

CJ sighed. "No secrets around here."

The only response she received was a toothy grin.

"Anything going on?" asked CJ.

"All quiet. Business will pick up after mid-terms." He paused. "Lieutenant Grimes changed our patrol procedures. We're to have only two patrol cars manned and the rest of the third shift officers are to patrol on foot. Some grumbled, but nothing serious."

"The lieutenant was only following orders. The chief and I decided this morning to increase foot patrols at night. It's amazing how much more you can see and hear if you're not in a car. I'm glad to see you out on foot."

Ramirez, dressed in only a light jacket, shivered. "Not for long. Certain privileges come with rank."

CJ countered. "It also has its headaches. Who else is patrolling in a car?"

"The officers are rotating. They drive for two hours and stay on foot the other six. I told them to work it out among themselves when they would be in the patrol car."

CJ opened the door to her vehicle. "I'm going to make a loop through campus and go home. Call if anything breaks loose, especially if there's another stolen car."

The campus settled into sleep mode. After finishing her tour of the west side of campus, she started on the east. This brought her to a tight cluster of academic buildings. She looped around them at a crawl with lights off. Nothing of consequence. The next street brought her in front of one of the cafeterias. She'd almost passed it when she noticed the second patrol car at the rear of the building, a lousy place to look for a car thief.

CJ pulled to the curb in front of the cafeteria and set off on foot. She looped around the building and came up on the rear of the patrol car. Several minutes passed, and the driver didn't move. She eased forward with cell phone in hand, ready to record. The lighting wasn't conducive for filming, but she decided it was better than nothing.

After recording, she gave a swift rap on the window. The driver's head snapped forward. He slicked back his hair, opened his door and stepped out.

"Enjoying your nap, Officer Sloan?" asked CJ.

"I wasn't sleeping."

CJ held up her cell phone. "Want to see the video?"

His fist clenched into a ball. He'd been caught, but it wasn't in his nature to deny responsibility or guilt, especially to her.

His hand relaxed. "This is exactly what I'd expect from you. Chief Sylvester is in the hospital and that makes you the acting chief. So what do you do? You come hunting for me. You never come to campus this late."

CJ stepped around Sloan and grabbed the microphone in his car. "ACU 02 to 09."

"Go ahead 02," said Sgt. Ramirez.

"Come to the delivery entrance of the east campus cafeteria."

"10-04."

As soon as CJ stepped from the car, Sloan laughed. "What are you going to do? Tell that lazy sergeant I've been a bad boy?" His face grew darker in the harsh light coming from the loading dock. "I don't care what you do. I'm sick of you and this place. This isn't a police department, it's a babysitting service to a bunch of rich kids."

CJ shook her head. "Don't make this worse than it is."

"Or what? What are you going to do? Fire me?" He took a step forward and lowered his voice. "For your information, I turned in my notice tonight. This is my last week." His chest ballooned out. "This time next week I'll be working with a real police department." His eyelids narrowed to slits. "You'd better be careful coming through town. I don't take kindly to speeders or people who run stop signs."

CJ took a step forward herself. "Are you threatening me, Officer Sloan?"

A crooked smile pulled up one side of his top lip. "I'm asking you to drive safe."

CJ pulled out her cell phone and held it so he could see. "I've been recording our conversation. You'd better hope you have a job working for the city. If you don't, the chances of you being unemployed are increasing with every word you say."

Sgt. Ramirez' arrival put an end to further discussion.

"Sergeant," said CJ. "Officer Sloan is having trouble keeping his eyes open in the patrol car. Don't you think it would be best if he finished the rest of his shift on foot?"

Ramirez signaled for Sloan to take off by jerking his head to one side.

The sergeant's radio crackled to life. "Dispatch to ACU 09."

"Go ahead," said Sergeant Ramirez.

"Meet a male student in parking lot of library. It's regarding a possible vehicle theft."

CJ moaned.

Sloan laughed as he stepped into the night.

CHAPTER TEN

"You look a little rough around the edges," said David.

Dawn's light streamed into the breakfast nook as CJ pulled a tattered terrycloth robe tight. A cup of black stimulant sat in front of her with steam billowing upward.

"It was a lousy night. I didn't have a jacket and paid the price when I went to investigate another missing car."

David raised his gaze up from the pan of frying bacon. "Another? Last night?"

"It was early this morning. You were sucking the paint off the walls with your snoring by the time I made it home. I grabbed a blanket and caught a couple hours rest on the couch."

A sip of coffee caused her to grimace. David's raised eyebrows asked what was wrong without words.

"Sore throat," said CJ. She took another sip. "How can I say this without sounding snobbish?" She ran her finger around the rim of the mug. "An economically disadvantaged man and his sons came to the hospital visiting room after you left. The children weren't the picture of hygiene or health.

They may have infected me with something that would make penicillin turn and run in fear."

David pulled crisp bacon from the pan and dabbed it with paper towels. "It's probably a cold from standing in the night air."

The hot coffee did little to sooth her throat. "Could you put two pieces of bread in the toaster for me?"

"No eggs this morning?"

"Toast is all that sounds good."

CJ took another sip and changed the subject. "Before the car went missing, I caught Sloan taking a nap in his patrol car. We had a difference of opinion concerning his effectiveness as an officer. The good news is, he turned in his resignation. This will be his last week."

David cracked two eggs and released them into hot grease. "I heard Sloan's going to work for the city. The change might be what he needs."

CJ wanted to say his leaving would justify a celebration, but she crammed down the words and moved on to another topic. "Have you checked on John this morning?"

David spoke as he flipped the eggs. "I sent a text to Dotty. She said his condition hasn't changed. They tried to take him off the ventilator, but he was too weak to breathe on his own. They'll try again later today."

The half-cup of Columbian dark roast tasted like boiled tree bark. She rose from the table and walked behind David as he scooped his over-medium eggs onto a plate. She gave him a behind-the-back hug and released him. "I'm hoping a scalding hot shower will kill whatever germs that yard urchin sprayed on me last night. I hope you've already showered. There won't be any hot water left when I'm through."

"I hope you're not going to work today." David stopped long enough to take in CJ's scowl. "Forget I said that."

CJ turned toward the bedroom, but David stopped her. "I have some good news."

"Oh?"

"Dad received a phone call from George Hewitt at First National yesterday morning. George must have caught wind of the money Dad's getting from the state and didn't want a million dollars going anywhere else. He offered Dad a loan. Dad jumped on it and even took George to lunch. He now has his own checking account and debit card. He's already come over for coffee and was making bad dad jokes."

"I wonder how George found out?" asked CJ with a straight face. She turned toward the bedroom as a grin parted her lips.

The grin left faster than it arrived. Another stolen car meant a phone call to Alice she didn't want to make.

MORE GOOD NEWS AWAITED CJ WHEN SHE ARRIVED AT work. Last night's missing car had been located safe and sound in the parking lot of an apartment complex close to campus. Some fraternity brothers decided it would be fun to take a pledge's car and relocate it.

With John in the hospital, CJ delegated the non-theft to her detective. She took a break to get a cup of tea. While walking back to her office, the front door flew open. Firm words came from Maria as she entered the building, escorting three young men with Greek letters on their windbreakers.

Maria directed them to an interview room, told them a camera and microphone would record them, and slammed the door. A smile of self-satisfaction pulled up the corners of her mouth. No one had activated the camera behind the one-way glass.

CJ crooked an index finger, and the detective followed.

"Shut the door, Maria."

The diminutive woman with large black eyes and raven hair settled in a chair. She didn't weigh more than a hundred and ten pounds, but CJ had seen her fight in mixed martial arts bouts. David described her as being tough as a fifty-cent steak.

"Are those our would-be car thieves?"

Maria nodded. "More like the three stooges. I thought about slapping cuffs on them, but the tall one started crying when I told them to get in the car. They're not bad kids. Just an attack of stupid."

A sneeze rose in CJ, but she quelled it before it exploded. Maria's gaze fixed on her, followed by an unequivocal statement. "You're sick."

"I don't have time to be sick."

"That's something Chief Sylvester would say. Look where he is."

CJ didn't have a comeback, so she changed the subject. "What are you going to do with the three joy-riders?"

"I'll fill out the report and go heavy on how it was a prank, and make it clear they cooperated." She issued a sly smile. "But I won't tell them that. I get a kick out of putting the fear of God in kids that forget their parents sent them here to get an education."

CJ waved a hand at Maria. "Enjoy the counseling session. I need to call President Cummings and tell her last night's theft was a false alarm."

The phone call to Alice didn't go as planned. She'd already sent out an email to the regents informing them of Chief Sylvester's medical condition and of another missing car. Alice received a reply from the chairman saying he was calling an emergency meeting of the regents to take place Monday morning. CJ was to attend if Chief Sylvester couldn't. She counted the days on the calendar. Only three days to catch a car thief.

Along with the unwelcome news of CJ having to meet with the regents, some good news came that afternoon concerning the Chief. He was breathing on his own.

By the end of the day, CJ's throat felt as if eighty-grit sandpaper had rubbed it raw. She'd run out of tissues and resorted to using toilet paper. Her body ached and all she could think of was getting home and in bed.

CHAPTER ELEVEN

"I've seen you look better," said David as he looked up from the desk of his home office.

"Thanks. I've felt better." CJ glanced at the pages scattered across his desk. "Is this the data on the car thefts?"

"Yeah. Do you want to see what I've found?"

"Not now. I need sleep. The board of regents called a meeting for Monday morning. With John in the hospital, I'm on the hot seat. I'll be heading back to work tonight."

David stood, stretched, and settled back in his chair. "Speaking of John, I heard from Dotty. He's running a fever. It looks like you'll be the acting chief for the foreseeable future."

CJ snatched a tissue from the desk in time to catch a sneeze and gave her nose a productive blow. David asked, "Do you think it's wise for you to go back to work tonight?"

"I have to. All supervisors are working four-hour night shifts this weekend. That includes me. An arrest of a car thief would go a long way to salvaging our new building, not to mention John's job." She paused. "I hadn't thought of this, but it may be my job that's on the line. If they're looking for someone to blame, they don't care if it's the chief or the assistant chief."

"Don't borrow trouble."

CJ turned to leave. "I want to hedge our chances. At least they won't be able to accuse me of not doing all I can."

Another sneeze erupted. This time she caught it in the crook of her elbow.

"Get to bed. I'll bring you some soup," said David.

CJ waved her hand as a sign that she wanted nothing to eat. "I just want to crash. Make sure I'm up at one o'clock. My shift is two until dawn."

She took a step but turned. "Could you bring a copy of your report by my office in the morning?"

David's eyebrows lifted upward. "Are you planning on working all day tomorrow?"

"Till noon. The regents want reports to examine."

"Ah," said David. "Dad and I are going to Dallas tomorrow. He found a car he wants to buy on the internet."

CJ would have continued the conversation but her fatigued body screamed for rest. Another sneeze sealed her wordless departure.

———

A COOL SOUTH WIND BLEW RESTLESS CLOUDS NORTHWARD beginning in the early hours of Saturday morning. Instead of taking the smart way out and riding in her unmarked Chevy Tahoe, CJ wanted to set an example. Dressed like a coed in jeans, a black hoody and hiking boots, she set out on foot. Lurking in the shadows and scanning parking lots for suspicious activity, the chills attacked with regularity.

After thirty motionless minutes in each spot, CJ moved

on to the next place to watch and listen. Her mind wandered as she fought off sneezes. Officer Sloan had called in sick. She should have expected it. He'd already used up all his accrued leave time, except for eight hours. His last-minute call angered her all the same.

Halfway through her shift, Sergeant Ramirez tried to convince her to get out of the night air and patrol with him. She turned him down. Some deep-seated sense of duty told her not to expect more from her officers than she gave.

The sergeant returned twenty minutes later with a cup of coffee and an apple fritter. Throat lozenges gave the coffee a taste that reminded her of mouthwash, but she drank it anyway. She pitched the pastry in a dumpster behind a dorm after two bites.

First light ended the eventless night. Gray clouds scuttled northward, laden with gulf moisture, a portent of rains to come. Most likely they'd soak Oklahoma, or perhaps further north. Nothing but humidity for Central Texas. At least that's what the weatherman promised.

David and his father arrived at her office at seven o'clock with orange juice, daytime cold and flu medicine and multiple capsules of vitamin C. The juice burned the back of her throat, but the cool made it a good burn.

"Quiet night?" asked David after he and his father made themselves comfortable in the chairs facing her desk.

"Um. Two traffic stops and one student throwing up on the steps of the men's athletic dorm. Sergeant Ramirez handled the up-chucker."

"Drunk or sick?" asked David.

CJ shrugged. "Either way, I'm glad I wasn't there. The smell wouldn't have set well with me."

Bob said, "You should go home."

As much as she longed to get back in their king bed and

sleep for two days, CJ shook her head. "I can't. If I don't get this report started today, something will break loose and I'll be standing in front of the regents with nothing but a blank sheet of paper in my hand and a stupid look on my face."

Pointing to the pack of medicine, David said, "I got you the non-drowsy formula. Come home as soon as you can."

"I hope it has something for a cough in it."

He gave her a hard stare. "You're not working tonight, are you?"

She nodded. "From ten until two." She flicked a hand as if that could remove his scowl. "Don't worry. I'll sleep tomorrow."

She cast her gaze on her father-in-law. "Why are you going all the way to Dallas to look at a car?"

"I can't find what I'm looking for locally." He reached in a manila folder he'd brought with him and pulled out the screenshot of a car with all the pertinent information included.

"A used car?" asked CJ.

Bob's smile lit up his face. "Most of the men in prison kept pictures of women on the walls of their cells. I looked at a color glossy of a 1970 Chevelle SS 396 every day for fourteen of the last sixteen years. I always wanted a car like this one, even when I was in high school. Life happened, and I never scratched the itch." He pointed to the photo on the page. "They claim this beauty is fully restored. If it's legit, I'll drive it home today."

David rose and gave her a look of concern. "Get home and to bed as soon as you can."

One minor crisis followed another, and she dragged herself through the back door of their home at four thirty. She shucked off her clothes and tugged on a football jersey. The duvet came up to her chin before she realized she hadn't brushed her teeth. They remained unbrushed until she rose for the night shift. Four more hours of work tonight and then she'd catch up on her sleep.

At least, that was the plan.

CHAPTER TWELVE

Four hours of skulking in the dark yielded no trace of anyone interested in stealing a car, or anything else. CJ hacked and coughed her way through the shift until Maria relieved her at 2:00 a.m. Traveling home, she noted that all she'd accomplished was to make her cold worse. Beads of perspiration popped up on her forehead, but her body felt like a block of ice. Perhaps she could sweat it out under a hot shower if her condition hadn't improved by the time she woke up in the evening.

She calculated the number of hours available before she was to appear before the board of regents. Thirty hours would give her plenty of time to rest and kick the cold.

A scouring of the bathroom cabinets revealed no cough syrup. Never mind, she couldn't keep her eyes open another minute. A restless sleep followed, interrupted by spasms of coughing. Daylight poured in through a crack in the drapes, acting like a spotlight on her face in an otherwise dark bedroom.

David returned from a mid-morning mercy trip to town with a large bottle of cough syrup. Another interruption, but this one she welcomed. She'd settled into a deep sleep when her phone rang.

"Yeah," she croaked.

"Is that you, CJ?"

The voice belonged to Lieutenant Page.

CJ grabbed another pillow and stuffed it under her head. "What's wrong?"

"You'd better get up here. We have a report of a female student abduction."

She sat straight up, rubbing grit from her eyes with her free hand. "Are you sure it's an abduction?"

"Looks like it to me, but it was dusk when it happened. A student filmed the incident with her phone from her dorm room. Three guys jumped out of a car and grabbed a girl wearing an ACU sweatshirt. One held a pistol and the other two put a black sack over her head. They shoved her in the back seat and took off."

By the time Lieutenant Page finished the report, CJ had a pair of slacks stripped from a hanger and was pulling up the zipper. "Have you notified city and county?"

"Done."

"What time is it?"

"6:05 p.m."

"Call in all third shift supervisors and officers scheduled to work tonight. Also, get Maria on it. Do you have the car's description?"

"Tan Honda Civic, about four or five years old."

CJ shook her head. "There's a million of those. What about plates?"

"The angle of the cell phone was lousy. I'm pulling up video from around campus to see if we can get lucky."

"Get an officer off patrol to help you. I'll be there in ten minutes." She choked back a cough. "Have you called President Cummings?"

"Not yet."

"I'll call her. You find that car and the name of the student."

The phone call with Alice lasted mere seconds. The university president would meet her at the ACU police building.

CJ pushed the disconnect icon and tossed her phone on the bed. It landed at the same time a spasm of coughs doubled her over. The next thing she knew, David's hand was rubbing her back.

"I heard it on the scanner. You're not going in, are you?"

She didn't bother responding.

The wag of David's head showed he didn't like her silent answer, but he'd honor it. He retrieved her shoulder holster and Glock from the dresser. "You're in no condition to drive. I'll take you."

THE SAGACITY OF DAVID'S DECISION TO INSIST ON DRIVING soon proved out. All CJ could do on the ten-mile trip was cough and swig Formula 44D. By the time they arrived, she'd self-medicated to the tune of three times the recommended dosage. At least her cough quelled, if only temporarily.

David wheeled into Chief Sylvester's reserved parking spot, bringing his SUV alongside a pristine 1970 Chevelle SS.

"Someone took my spot," said CJ.

"That's Dad's new car. He called Alice and asked her if she wanted to get an ice cream cone."

CJ didn't have the time or inclination to process Bob and Alice reliving high school days. She burst through the front door of the campus police department and headed to John's office, where a blown-up map of the campus and an enlarged aerial photo of ACU hung on a wall. There she found Lieu-tenant Page, Alice and Maria.

"Show me," said CJ.

The lieutenant pointed to a spot on the map. "There's a street lamp in the parking lot right here."

CJ turned to Maria. "Have you seen the video?"

Maria nodded. "It's bumpy and grainy, but you can tell what's going on." She added, "It's gone viral."

"What! How?" CJ threw up her hands. "If it's viral, there's no un-ringing this bell. We need to focus."

CJ drew a circle on the map. "We're going to canvas everything and everyone in a two-block area of the abduc-tion. Lieutenant, you'll assign the officers as soon as they arrive."

"Maria, go to the scene and make sure it's secured. Then, scour the area."

Looking away from the map, CJ gave a general announce-ment. "If any officer finds anyone with any information, bring them here. Questions?"

"What about me looking at the video footage from cameras around campus?" asked the lieutenant.

CJ hesitated then decided. "Good idea. Is there a sergeant on duty?"

"Sergeant Ramirez is in the break room."

"Have him assign officers as they arrive."

The lieutenant handed her the cell phone containing the recording. "I sent you an email with the video. The girl who filmed it is in the interview room."

"Have you seen it on a bigger screen?"

"It's been a little busy."

A rattling cough came forth from CJ. She let it run its course and turned breathlessly to Alice. "Let's go to the break room. I'll grab my laptop."

The first thing CJ had to do when she reached the break

room was tear off a sheet from a roll of paper towels and blow her nose. She turned to David, who stood looking out a window into the parking lot. "Have you seen Sergeant Ramirez?"

David pointed to something outside the building. "Dad's showing him his new car."

A coughing spasm hit CJ.

It took David five long steps to reach CJ. "Sit down before you fall down. What do you want me to do?"

"Connect my laptop to the monitor on the wall."

In less than a minute David made the connections and started the video. The trio stared at a shaky image of a female walking across a shadowed parking lot and pausing under a street light. A car came upon her fast and braked hard. The images seemed to bounce as the person capturing the images gave narration that something seemed wrong.

Two hooded persons jumped from the passenger's side as a third exited from the back seat on the driver's side. One stood in front of the young woman with a pistol pointed at her. The victim appeared to be pinned to the spot in what must have been fear. In mere seconds the other two placed a black cloth sack over her head, duct taped her hands in front of her and hustled her into the car. The screen went black.

"I'll play it back," said David. He did so, stopping it every few seconds. He repeated this again. On the fourth time through, he stopped it as the car came to a sliding stop.

"This is odd," he said. "There's a car charging toward her and she turns around. She knows it's coming too fast, but she doesn't move."

"Too surprised?" asked CJ.

"Possible," said David. "But she doesn't offer any resistance or even lift her hands to keep those two from putting the sack over her face." He ran the film forward and stopped it again. "Look, they approached her from the front with the sack, not the rear."

"What are you saying?" asked Alice.

"He's saying this may be a hoax," said CJ.

David cupped a hand over his ear with an earbud inserted. A coiled wire stretched down to the radio in his jacket pocket. He listened and pulled out the earbud. "Highway patrol thinks they have the car spotted in Bell County. The trooper made the plates and reported the car has an ACU parking sticker. He backed off and is waiting for additional help before they perform a felony stop."

David's cell phone rang. "Yes, Sir."

CJ guessed it was Ranger Captain Crow.

"I'm at ACU with CJ. We've just reviewed the video of the possible abduction. I don't think it's a kidnapping."

David explained what they'd seen, nodded, and shoved the phone in his pocket. "I'm to go to Bell County and sort this out. Send me the video," he said over his shoulder.

Second guessing hit the second David left the room. Had she overreacted? What about the expense of overtime? Had she involved other agencies in a college prank?

An image of the smirking face of Chip Sloan flashed in front of her. He'd arrive any moment for his last day of work and mock her for incompetence.

Alice's touch on her forearm brought CJ back to the present. "Don't second guess yourself."

CJ stood and squared her shoulders. "Let's bring in the student who took this video. Something's going on and it's not an abduction."

CHAPTER THIRTEEN

By the time David returned at ten thirty, CJ thought a truck had run her over. A simple class assignment for a cinematography class had morphed into a multi-county alert with would-be thespians staring down the barrels of pistols, rifles and shotguns. Their return to campus came with profuse apologies for not notifying the campus police of their activities.

Thick, sticky night air closed in as soon as CJ opened the door to the University Police Department. Distant flashes of lightning gave warning of an approaching wet, cold front. Once again, the weatherman had underestimated the speed of the front. She hoped to be home before it hit. Needing rest to function at the regents' meeting the following day, she longed for relief from her cough and a full night's sleep.

David led the way to his SUV. She alternated her gaze between David's stride and the truck. Everything ached.

"Thanks for bringing me supper. Too bad I couldn't eat any of it. Anyway, the throat lozenges are helping," said CJ.

"If you don't get to bed, you'll be joining John in the hospital."

A chill shot through her. "I feel awful. It sprinkled last night when I was hiding in the bushes watching the parking lot between Mesquite Hall and the library."

"Go home now. And it's straight to bed with you."

She shook her head and grimaced. It pounded as if miners were wailing away with pickaxes, but she needed to finish preparing for tomorrow's meeting.

"You're one hard-headed woman," said David with a huff. "Stop worrying." He took a step closer and reached for her arm.

She held up a hand with an open palm. "Don't get too close. I don't want you getting whatever I have. After tomorrow's meeting, I'll be able to rest."

The first rumble of distant thunder rolled across the fields and through campus. Livestock from the Ag Department across the street made for the sanctuary of the lee side of barns. Another shiver shook CJ from head to waist.

Tires squealed as an older burgundy Camaro took a corner too fast and headed toward their location. A trailing patrol car activated pulsating red and blue lights. Both vehicles came to rest forty yards past the police department.

"Who's making the stop?" asked David.

"Sloan. It's his last day before he goes to work at Riverview P.D."

"At least you're getting rid of one problem."

She gave her head a slow nod as she kept her eyes on Sloan. He approached the driver. "You know, I tried to work with him, but..."

What sounded like a string of exploding firecrackers shattered the calm of the evening. Sloan slumped to the ground. The Camaro's tires smoked and screeched as they fought to gain traction. Sloan raised his pistol and fired a single round.

CJ had her .40 caliber Glock in her hand and was raising

it when David yelled, "Hold fire!" She glanced to her right to see him staring down the sights of his .357 caliber Model 19.

"Houses down range. Can't risk it," said David.

Obscured by trees lining the street, the sports car squealed around a corner and sped off campus.

CJ keyed her microphone. "ACU 02 to all units. Shots fired. Officer down. Repeat. ACU 02 to all units. Shots fired. Officer hit. Officer down. Roll EMS to ACUPD. Suspect vehicle is a burgundy Camaro. Approach with extreme caution. Suspect armed with fully automatic weapon."

By the time she finished her broadcast, she had sprinted halfway to where the officer lay. David's SUV flew past her with lights pulsing and siren screaming.

Sloan lay on his back, pistol held loose in his hand. Blood flowed from his right thigh and lower abdomen, and gushed from his neck.

"Tell EMS to step it up," shouted CJ into her microphone.

Her hands cupped over the worst of the wounds. She applied as much pressure as she could to the tear in his neck. Blood oozed from between her fingers as it pulsed against her palm. She dared not pull back her hands. Questioning eyes looked up at her.

Too much blood. It saturated and spread from his uniform into pools on the street. Its sticky dampness soaked her knees as she knelt beside him.

The pulsing slowed, then stopped. A last short exhale of breath. An unspoken question remained in Sloan's motionless gaze.

A metallic taste hit her. She might as well have been chewing aluminum foil. Vomit rose in her throat. She had to turn away from the smell or she'd contaminate the crime scene. Facing the stiffening wind preceding the storm, she managed not to retch.

How had it happened so fast? Why? A simple traffic stop

ended a life. Was he dead? Perhaps someone with more training and skill could revive him.

No. Unlike the student's film of an abduction, this was real. She'd watched an officer, her officer, die in front of her.

EMS made it to the scene in less than three minutes. Officer Charles 'Chip' Sloan had been dead for two of those minutes. Only after EMTs confirmed the obvious did she look at her blood-soaked hands. Nausea rose up in an undeniable wave. She clamped a hand over her mouth and moved away from the body. The heaving didn't stop until her already sore ribs hurt as much as her soul.

Mocking rain came in torrents. It took mere seconds before it soaked her down to her underwear and socks. Cold gusts from the season's first blue norther added another layer of misery. She faced the stinging rain and allowed it to wash away salty tears.

Yellow police barrier tape made a rectangle around a university patrol car and the immediate area. A silver thermal blanket covered the deceased officer. Maria Vasquez retrieved bottles of water and helped CJ wash most of the blood from her hands. She also wrapped CJ in an undersized raincoat and wrapped her again in another silver blanket. Police radios crackled, but the focus of CJ's gaze and attention remained on Sloan.

The hand of a state trooper rested on CJ's shoulder as she sat on the front bumper of Maria's car, her gaze locked. Another chill quaked her body.

The rain stopped as quick as it started, but the relentless north wind cut through the feeble layers Maria had wrapped around her.

The voice of a two-pack-a-day smoker pierced hushed

conversations. "I want this crime scene tape extended another twenty yards up and down the street."

CJ stood and observed the figure of Riverview's Chief of Police, Douglas 'Dutch' Satterfield, as he pointed to a city police officer. She rose from the bumper and approached the chief. He wore a brown Stetson with a crease that went out of style twenty years ago.

"What are you doing?" she asked.

Chief Satterfield hooked his thumbs in his belt and raised his nose, most likely to make it appear he was of equal height. "I'm taking over. You're out of your league. You don't have the experience or the resources to investigate a capital murder. The city already hired Officer Sloan." He pointed an index finger downward. "That makes him mine. The university falls within the city limits. It's in my jurisdiction."

Instead of retreating, CJ took a step forward, then another, close enough to see the red lines in the whites of Chief Satterfield's eyes. Her eyes narrowed, and she spoke through clenched teeth.

"Take a good look at that patrol car. It belongs to the police department of Agape Christian University." She then pointed down to the motionless form. "Under that blanket is an officer wearing the uniform of this university." She pointed toward the ground. "You're standing on university property." Her gaze locked on his right eye and didn't waver. "Don't you dare come here lecturing me on jurisdictions and accusing me of ineptitude when my officer is lying in his own blood. As for adequate resources, don't worry about that. I have it under control."

"I doubt that," snapped the Chief. "Your department doesn't have an experienced detective, let alone any forensic people. How are you going to process this crime scene?"

"That's why I'm here." The voice came from CJ's blind side.

A man stepped forward wearing a gray felt cowboy hat, white shirt, cowboy-cut sports coat, khaki pants and black lizard-skin boots. The circular badge on his chest reflected his identity and title: Captain, Texas Rangers. Stephen Crow looked at her and nodded. "CJ," he said in a flat voice.

Captain Crow's arm then went over the shoulder of Chief Satterfield. His soft voice held the pitch of someone speaking to an old friend. "Dutch, I was coming back from Austin when I caught the radio traffic. You know the Rangers will be front and center on any investigation that involves the death of an officer anywhere in the state. CJ called me and I notified our state forensic team to get up here on the double."

Radios came to life. A city officer called for backup and multiple units were responding. He'd spotted the suspect's vehicle at a Walgreen's parking lot on the other side of the interstate.

Captain Crow removed his hand from Chief Satterfield's shoulder. "Looks like there's a cop killer for you to apprehend. I'll stick around here and make sure the lab boys earn their keep."

All city units left university property in short order. Captain Crow moved toward the body and motioned for CJ to follow him. "You okay?"

She shrugged, "Yeah—sort of." The quiver in her voice showed there was more "sort of" than "yes."

"What am I going to see when I lift this silver sheet?" asked Captain Crow.

CJ took in a deep breath and spoke through chattering teeth. "A real mess. Full auto. Point blank. First shot entered upper right leg. Shots continued upward and to the right. At least two more rounds penetrated the abdomen below the vest. It stopped the rest except one to the throat that severed the artery." CJ looked down at her hands. Blood remained under her nails and rimmed her cuticles.

She pointed toward the police station. "David and I were standing outside watching the whole thing. Officer Sloan got off a shot, but he was down and the car was moving away fast."

"Did you shoot?"

She shook her head. "Neither did David. Houses down range. Also, we didn't know who else might be in the car."

CJ looked down at the motionless form. "Are you going to look?"

"Not now. You told me what I needed to know." He paused. "What kind of weapon do you think it was?"

"Definitely a full auto. From the sound, I'd say a 9 mm. Not a long gun in a car that small and at that angle. Something the size of an Uzi. Steering wheel would be in the way for anything bigger."

The Ranger captain looked toward the Ag building. "Full auto 9 mm pistols are favorites for gangs." He opened his mouth to say more, but his cell phone interrupted him. The conversation didn't last long. "That was David. Sloan's shot went through the driver's door and struck the guy in the leg. It shattered the femur and clipped the femoral artery. He passed out before officers arrived."

CJ nodded. "Dead?"

"Not yet. EMS got to him in time and he's on his way to the hospital. Guess what David saw when they cut the guy's shirt off?"

Her response came without hesitation. "Ink."

"Mexican Mafia tattoos." He gave her a long look. "I wish you hadn't turned down being a Ranger. Why don't you at least consider coming back to the highway patrol?"

"Thanks, but I can't think about that now." She gave him her full attention. "This isn't over for us, is it?"

"Cars are being stolen all over Central Texas." He looked away. "This confirms who's behind it."

CJ had one more question for the man who would have been her supervisor if she'd accepted the Ranger job offered last year. "Why did you tell Chief Satterfield I called and asked you to send the state forensic team?"

A sly smile crossed the countenance of the veteran lawman. "Did I say you called me? I keep getting you and David mixed up."

The next gust of frigid wind ripped the silver thermal blanket away and sent it sailing. CJ's knees buckled. Captain Crow took one arm and Maria grabbed the other and led CJ to Maria's car. She couldn't stop shaking. Was it from the cold or the thought of explaining this at tomorrow's board of regents meeting?

CHAPTER FOURTEEN

CJ made her way to the vacant seat at the far end of the rectangular table in President Cummings' office. She placed a stack of papers in front of her, clasped her hands together as a paperweight and waited for the room to stop spinning and the white floaty spots to clear from her vision.

"Assistant Chief Harper," began Chairman Darden. "Thank you for coming. Were you able to get any sleep last night?"

"No, Sir." Her voice cracked. The lozenge she worked over with her tongue did nothing to quell the burn in her throat.

"We'll try to keep this as brief as possible. Our original intent in asking you to attend this meeting was to clarify cost projections on the new police building. We also wanted an update on what's being done about the stolen cars. The events of last night have pushed the first discussion to the back burner. In fact, President Cummings is confident the lingering concerns any of us have regarding budget adjustments can be handled by e-mail. How does that sound?"

"That's fine, but since we turned in the original projections some things have changed. We now show—"

Before CJ could finish, a crow-like voice squawked from the far end of the table. "Just as I suspected." The name plate in front of the woman read Gloria Fishbaum. Close-cropped hair, the color of muddy water streaked by sunlight, framed a scowling face.

"I told you this would happen." Her speech reflected her features which included a thin angular nose, a sharp chin and ears bedecked with multiple diamond studs. "We committed to an unnecessary project and now we're told we must spend more. I don't see why you voted on giving a new palace for police officers. The academic needs far outweigh this budget buster."

CJ bit the inside of her lip. Her throat throbbed and the sharp words of Ms. Fishbaum brought back the miners for more pounding inside her head.

Chairman Darden tapped his pen on a legal pad as he responded. "Gloria, we discussed this at length. We examined the age and condition of the building and found it inadequate. The board examined everything presented by Chief Sylvester and President Cummings, and we voted."

He shifted his gaze. "CJ, you said something about changing the cost projections?"

Alice spoke up. "I'm pleased to report we've reduced the cost projections. Chief Sylvester recruited the leading service fraternity on campus to do all the painting for the renovations. The fraternity's connections with a paint company resulted in us being able to purchase supplies at less than wholesale. The chief has also enlisted other campus organizations to help with clean up and disposal of waste at the job site that will result in additional savings."

"I guess that caps the well," said Chairman Darden. "Let's keep things moving forward and hear first-hand what happened last night. CJ, the floor is all yours." He paused. " Is it all right if we call you CJ? Assistant Chief Harper is too much of a mouthful. "

A nod preceded a scratchy, "CJ is fine."

She relayed details of the crime in a straightforward manner, leaving out the more gruesome parts. Nearing the end of her report, the same fingernail-on-chalkboard voice interrupted her.

"Hold on a minute," said Ms. Fishbaum. "Why did the officer stop the car?"

"Our working hypothesis is Officer Sloan might have noticed the student parking decal displayed on the wrong side of the rear window. Our officers are under instructions to stop cars when they observe this and tell the students to peel it off and reapply it correctly. Citations aren't issued, only instructions."

"Do you think that's a wise policy? It seems a minor infraction like this should be handled in a way that is less confrontational. Why not send the student an e-mail?"

CJ fought to keep a tone of frustration out of her voice. "You used the word confrontational. We train our officers to change that perception. I'm under no illusion that traffic stops can escalate to confrontations, but they can also be opportunities to interact in ways that are a positive experience. That's our goal."

Pursed lips showed only partial satisfaction with the answer. Ms. Fishbaum moved on with another question. "Do you believe the Texas Rangers will do a thorough job of investigating this incident?"

"I have complete confidence in them."

"I don't know." The woman's eyebrows pinched together. "Perhaps we should explore hiring an independent investigative agency to look into this."

Billy Paul spoke up with a one-word question. "Why?"

"What are you asking, Mr. Stargate?"

"Why pay twice? A minute ago, you were going on about money. Now you're ready to spend it like it was water."

"I'm concerned about litigation."

"Who from?" Billy Paul leaned forward. "The man that did the shooting is a gang member. I can't see them rushing to defend him. Seems to me you're borrowing trouble."

Ms. Fishbaum leaned forward. "Has it been established that the Hispanic male was a member of a gang?"

CJ answered, "He has the tattoos and—"

Ms. Fishbaum didn't let her finish. "I'm sensing this may be racial profiling."

Conversations ran together. Chairman Darden entered the fray as Gloria Fishbaum raised her voice to an unbearable screech. "We're getting off subject. We can discuss policy after we hear the facts."

"Current policies may have contributed to this mess," said Ms. Fishbaum, "What could this officer have done to avoid this situation?" Her black-framed eyeglasses fastened in the middle. She pulled them apart and let them dangle around her neck. "Enrollment will suffer because of the publicity this incident will bring."

Gloria Fishbaum may have loved the sound of her own voice, but CJ had heard all of it she could stand. "Ms. Fishbaum, a veteran highway patrol officer and I witnessed the event. We discussed the incident at length with a captain of the Texas Rangers. All three of us concluded we would have approached the vehicle as Officer Sloan did."

Ms. Fishbaum lifted her chin. "I can't accept that. The reputation of the university hangs on this campus being a place where parents can send their children without the fear of bullets being sprayed around campus. Perhaps you and these so-called veteran lawmen are not properly trained in ways of diffusing volatile situations."

CJ didn't respond. Instead, she rose and pushed her chair to an open spot ten feet from the table. "Ms. Fishbaum, will you assist me in a demonstration? I promise it won't take long and I believe you and the board members will find it informative."

"I have no intention of participating in whatever theatrics you have in mind."

Billy Paul jumped to his feet. "I'll do it."

"Thank you, Mr. Stargate. Please stand by President Cummings' desk."

Billy Paul moved to a spot several yards behind the chair and stood waiting for instructions. CJ settled herself facing the long side of the conference table. The back of the chair hid her torso from Billy Paul. All members arranged themselves so they had an unobstructed view of the demonstration.

CJ spoke over her shoulder. "Mr. Stargate, you are Officer Sloan. You've noticed a traffic violation and you've activated your emergency lights. The tinted back glass of the Camaro, headrests and the upswept trunk make it difficult to see if anyone is in the back seat. The driver's headrest restricts your view of the operator. You come closer. The driver's window whirls down and you see an elbow."

Out of sight from Billy Paul, but in clear view of the board of regents, CJ formed her right hand into the shape of a pistol.

"Walk toward me, Officer Sloan. Remember, this is a routine traffic stop of a car you believe is occupied by a university student. The only thing you know they have done wrong involves taking a corner a little fast, and a misplaced parking sticker."

As Billy Paul reached CJ's left elbow she hollered, "BANG! BANG! BANG!"

The shouts caused several to flinch, including Ms. Fishbaum.

CJ was on her feet. "No, Officer Sloan. You're no longer standing."

Billy Paul played the part and slumped to the carpet.

CJ picked up the pace and volume of her narrative. "In one full second—" She turned to the regents. "Everyone, repeat after me. 'One.'"

Most of the regents repeated the phrase.

CJ turned back to the prostrate man. "In one second, ten rounds struck you from an automatic Tech 9 machine pistol. The first bullet shattered your hip and two rounds tore through your abdomen. Your Kevlar vest stopped five rounds but knocked you breathless, broke ribs, and bruised your torso. Recoil from the gun brought the muzzle higher as the rounds raked your body." With her hand still formed as a pistol, CJ jerked it upward and to the right. "One more round entered your body from a gun capable of firing six hundred rounds a minute. The last bullet ripped open your neck."

CJ turned back and faced the regents. "It took one second. Officer Sloan is no longer standing. He's on the ground gasping for air as life drains from him."

CJ turned to the now mute lawyer. "Put yourself in Officer Sloan's place, Ms. Fishbaum. One second. You're dying. Why didn't Sloan say or do something to change the outcome? Is it because he wasn't trained in proper intervention techniques?" She issued a stare she hoped would drive the woman from her world of fantasy. "What training do you suggest I give our officers that would have changed the outcome?"

The question went unanswered as the hush of death itself fell on the room.

CJ turned to the regents. "I'll tell you what kind of training I'm interested in giving my officers. Even as he died,

Charles Sloan drew his weapon and fired a single round at his killer. That instinctive reaction comes only from training."

She focused again on the defiant countenance of Gloria Fishbaum. "Let me fill you in on Raul Vargas, the man who murdered Officer Sloan. He's a member of the Mexican Mafia, a cartel that specializes in drugs, extortion, illegal weapons and violence of a nature far beyond most people's comprehension. Mr. Vargas is a two-time alumnus of our state's prison. Every time he goes to prison, he does his time in special housing because he's a confirmed gang member. They've deported him twice, but he finds his way back."

CJ pushed her chair back to its place but didn't sit down. "One more thing. The weapon he used was illegally modified from semi-automatic to full-auto. It's a favorite hobby of gangs."

Billy Paul voiced a question as he returned to his seat. "Do you think all the car thefts are linked to the Mexican Mafia?"

"My gut tells me yes. They found a copy of a key in the car's ignition."

"A key? How did they get a key?" asked Chairman Darden.

"That's what the Texas Rangers, the county sheriff, Riverview's chief of police and I will discuss." CJ looked at her watch. "Twenty-two minutes from now."

Ms. Fishbaum found her voice. "I don't want to minimize anything you've said, but I'm having a hard time imagining bucolic Riverview, Texas and this campus as being a hotbed of gang activity."

The headache and the rawness in her throat intensified as CJ circled the conference table. She bent her knees and looked eye to eye with the woman she now counted as a dangerous adversary. "Ms. Fishbaum, do you see the scar that runs from the corner of my eye to my ear?" She didn't expect, nor did she receive, a response. "The scar is from a jail key. On a bucolic county road not too far north of here, a member of a rather notorious motorcycle gang wanted to rape and kill me because I'm a woman and I wore the uniform of a state trooper. I shot and killed that man. If the circumstances were the same, I'd do it again. I look at this scar every day. It reminds me there are evil people who do wicked things, regardless of the setting."

CJ stood and reached out her hands with her palms down. "I hope everyone can see from where you're sitting. Notice how pink the cuticles are? They're stained with the blood of Officer Charles Sloan. I've washed them a dozen times and it won't come off." She looked down on Gloria Fishbaum. "Bucolic or not, evil came to this campus and to this part of the state. It won't leave until it's ripped out by the roots. So, if you'll excuse me, and even if you won't, I'm going to join a group of people who know how to deal with vermin."

Alice followed her out the door. "CJ, stop."

She turned and looked down on the woman who seemed taller than she was. Two petite hands lifted CJ's right hand. Alice kissed the back of her hand. She repeated her actions on her left hand.

"Go to your meeting," said Alice. "Get some sleep as soon as you can, but come see me tomorrow. We're all counting on you."

CHAPTER FIFTEEN

"What do you mean Captain Crow went home?" A vein in Chief Satterfield's forehead bulged. "He's the one that came in last night acting all high-and-mighty and took over my crime scene. He also asked us all to be here this morning." The chief looked at his watch. "We're ten minutes late. What's the holdup?"

David fielded the question with shoulders square and eyes fixed. "I didn't say Captain Crow went home. He's in Waco, testifying in a church arson case." David leaned back in his chair, trying to look the picture of relaxed authority. "CJ's on her way. We'll start as soon as she arrives.

"In the meantime," said David. "They've processed the crime scenes. As soon as I receive the results, or even partial results, I'll email them to you."

Sheriff Gladstone, a man of sixty-two and a former lieutenant with the highway patrol, glanced over his glasses. "David, are you in charge of this case?"

"Captain Crow will assign a Ranger today. I'm to be his right-hand man in Riverview."

"I still don't like it," mumbled Chief Satterfield.

The door opened, saving David from saying something he might regret. CJ mumbled an apology as she took a seat at the table, leaving as much space as she could from the men who'd congregated on one end.

"None of you want whatever I've got," said CJ.

"I'll vouch for that," said David as he noticed beads of sweat on CJ's forehead and top lip. A spasm of coughs doubled her over, and she took a swig from a brown bottle she dug out of her purse.

"Captain Crow and I made a list of things we need from each of you," said David. "I'll need copies of all reports on stolen vehicles for the last twelve months. I'll be doing a statistical analysis looking for patterns."

"I've already done that," said Chief Satterfield.

"Good. That will make my job easier. I've been compiling data for some time, but not all departments have been forthcoming. We already know the university has the highest number of stolen cars in the last two months, but the theft last night was different."

"How so?" asked the sheriff.

"Three things," said David. "The thief is a confirmed gang member. A key was used to open and start the car." He looked down at a list. "And one final item. The Camaro is equipped with OnStar tracking."

The sheriff let out a low whistle.

"What does that tell you, Sheriff?" asked David.

"They're able to open and start the cars in seconds without attracting attention. Then they're taking the cars someplace close by to disable the tracking."

"That's next on the list. Who in the city or county has the know-how and space to hide a car long enough to disable tracking devices?"

"That could be any home with a garage," said Chief Satterfield.

"True, but where are they taking them that doesn't attract suspicion, and what are they doing with the cars after they steal them? I see two possibilities. They can either strip them nearby, or haul them someplace else."

"That leaves a big haystack to find a needle in," said the sheriff.

CJ continued to rub her temples. She mopped her brow with the sleeve of her blouse.

"CJ, what steps are you taking on campus?" asked David.

Her head began a slow roll. "What?"

"I asked what you plan to do about the car thefts."

"I... uh..."

"Are you all right?"

She struggled to her feet. "Sore throat and..."

Her knees buckled as if a giant wave had hit her. Down she came, her head striking the edge of the table with something between a *crack* and a *thunk*.

By the time David reached her, blood pooled on the carpet of Chief Satterfield's conference room.

"Get a towel," shouted David to anyone who'd respond.

Sheriff Gladstone, already on his radio, called for EMS. Chief Satterfield stood and walked to the door, where he hollered for help.

A pencil-thin city patrolman appeared.

"Get towels, and be quick about it," said the Chief. "And find the janitor. This carpet is brand new."

"THERE YOU ARE. HOW WAS YOUR NAP?"

The familiarity of David's voice didn't match the setting. Lights, bright as those on a landing commercial jet, illumined a room full of sounds and smells incongruent to the office of Chief Satterfield.

CJ struggled to raise herself on the bed, but David's hands on her shoulders pinned her. She relaxed back onto a pillow. "Where am I?" Eyes refused to open more than a slit and her head pounded.

"Emergency room," she heard David say.

"What am I doing here?" Her voice cracked and didn't rise above a whisper.

"You, my love, have strep throat, a dandy sinus infection and you're exhausted. You also have three stitches in that pretty head of yours."

She lifted a hand and touched a bandage high on her forehead, inside the hairline. News of a fresh scar brought the world into focus. "If I keep it up, I'll look like the bride of Frankenstein."

"Don't worry. Your hair will cover this one."

CJ moaned. "How long have I been here?"

"A few hours."

"When can I leave?" Once more she tried to sit up, only to repeat her previous failure. "I have to be in President Cummings' office tomorrow morning."

David's head swung left to right. "You're off work, at least for the next three days."

"My officers. I need to..."

David's hand gave hers a light squeeze. "That's all taken care of. Captain Crow assigned Blake Cruz to the case. He and I are meeting with your officers in the morning along with Lieutenant Page. He's the acting chief until you get back to work. We'll give them the big picture at 6:00 a.m. Alice will be there too."

CJ tried to swallow, but it seemed her throat was not only aflame but swollen shut.

"Water?" asked David.

She nodded. The cold fluid soothed and burned at the same time. "I'm such a mess."

A doctor breezed through the blue curtains surrounding the bed. She pulled a computer stand toward her and logged in. After tucking her shoulder-length black hair behind an ear, she turned toward CJ. "Mrs. Harper, how are you feeling?"

"Rotten. My throat feels like someone poured gasoline down it and struck a match."

An unconcerned, "Uh-huh," came from the woman. "What else? Headache?"

"Throbbing."

The woman took a pen light, shone it in each of CJ's eyes and spoke as she administered the torture. "I understand you had a very long and trying day yesterday. How long were you awake?"

"I didn't sleep at all yesterday, or today until..."

"And before that?"

David spoke for her. "She averages seven hours a night. For the past week she struggled to get three to four."

"Coffee? Energy drinks?"

"Ounces or gallons per day?" said David.

The doctor returned to the keyboard and started typing. "We're going to monitor you for the next several hours. That's normal procedure for a head injury. If you're clear to leave, you won't have to worry about staying awake tonight. I'm ordering something for you we tested on Sleeping Beauty." She turned to David. "No kisses until late tomorrow night."

CJ shifted on the bed. "Why does my hip hurt?"

"I gave you a shot for strep throat. It has the consistency of cold honey. Hurts like crazy, but works great. You should be much improved by the time you wake up tomorrow. After that, a couple days of taking it easy and ten days of a strong antibiotic and you'll be good as new."

The same wind that blew the intern in carried her away.

CJ looked up at David. "Sore head, sore throat and a sore

caboose. I can't cook and I'm a lousy acting chief of police. I'm too tall and my scar count is going up. Why would a man like you want a woman like me?"

David raised his shoulders and let them fall. "It must be something from my childhood." He leaned over and kissed her forehead. "I always wanted to kiss Sleeping Beauty, but I'm drawing the line at having those six short guys live with us."

She reached up with the hand not encumbered by an IV and cupped his chin. "You need to work on your fairy tales before our children come along. There's seven short guys."

David smiled until CJ pushed harder on his cheeks and said. "Everything changed last night. It's personal. I'll not tolerate people coming on my turf and committing capital murder. I don't care how long it takes, I'll..."

"We," said David. He took her hand and she allowed her head to sink into the pillow. "I hear you, but this is bigger than just you. It's going to take a team to put a dent in the Mexican Mafia. And you'll be a star player." He paused. "But not until you get well."

CHAPTER SIXTEEN

Creeping into the bedroom unnoticed hadn't been a problem for the past twenty hours. David looked down at CJ. She'd made a quarter turn on the bed while he'd been at work and now lay with her mouth half open, inhaling and exhaling with deep breaths. His plopping down beside her resulted in her left eye opening enough to let him know she recognized his presence. A marked improvement from when he left that morning.

"How's the throat?" he asked after she'd straightened herself and settled on pillows he fluffed for her.

"Still sore." She cast her gaze to the nightstand and pointed at a glass. "Water and the big pill."

He retrieved them and watched as she swallowed and grimaced.

"What time is it?" asked CJ.

"Night. After ten."

She pushed herself up a little straighter. "I don't remember coming home last night or much of today except Bea and Alice stopping in to check on me. I can't tell you anything they said."

"I had to carry you in. Dad checked on you every hour and sent me a report via text."

CJ's hand found his.

"Bea left a pot of chicken noodle soup that Yari made for you. Are you hungry?"

"I'll try a little, but first, tell me how it went today."

"The campus is in shock. Your officers were somber this morning, but smoldering under the surface. You won't have a problem with them being alert and diligent."

"No stolen cars?"

"Nothing local, but one from Bastrop and one from a hotel parking lot in Bell County."

CJ looked past him. "They'll lie low and let the heat around here simmer down."

Instead of following that thread, David said, "Alice told me about your meeting with the board of regents."

CJ groaned.

"That bad?"

"Worse. One of the new board members rides a broom."

David couldn't help but chuckle.

"I'm serious," said CJ. "She's looking for scalps and I have a full head of hair." She raised her hand to her stitches. "At least I used to. Did Gloria Fishbaum sneak in the hospital and take a sample?"

"I'll get your soup," said David.

"Hurry. I'll be in another world when that pill kicks in."

AFTER A SECOND NIGHT OF UNINTERRUPTED SLEEP, CJ determined her health had improved enough to allow a shower. She dressed in a set of grey sweats with plenty of room to stretch, and slipped her feet in worn, but serviceable, house shoes.

Brunch in the breakfast nook consisted of a rerun of chicken noodle soup, toast and an antibiotic. She considered coffee, but the gurgle in her stomach convinced her otherwise.

Her spoon clanked into the empty bowl as a tow truck rounded the corner behind their house. It clattered as it turned toward the barn, and swung into the pasture. From there it backed up to the open barn doors and didn't stop until only the nose of the wrecker protruded.

Scurrying to the mud/laundry room, CJ traded her house shoes for scuffed work boots. A Farm Bureau baseball cap, scarf and brown corduroy jacket completed the mismatched ensemble. By the time she reached the barn, the tow truck driver had lowered the front end of yesteryear's Detroit dream to all-fours. Her father-in-law scribbled his name on a page, and the driver nodded a greeting as he passed her.

"What's this?" asked CJ as her father-in-law examined his prize that had seen much better days... and nights.

Bob Harper swept a hand over the rust-dappled hood. "It's the start of my second new business." He paused. "The first doesn't pay, but the benefits are terrific."

CJ held up her hands. "Slow down, Dad. What new businesses?"

"Come with me," he said.

They bypassed the rusting hulk and walked to the shiny Chevelle SS. Bob lifted the hood. "The restoration guys did a decent job, but they didn't pay attention to details. It runs, but not like it should." He stabbed an index finger at the radiator. "Look at that. It's old as the hills and gummed up. I have to drive slow to keep it from overheating."

He moved past the headlight and leaned over with hands on knees. "Look down the side. The fit and finish on this old girl isn't up to my standards."

He let out a sigh. "Serves me right for being in such a hurry."

Bob stood and focused on CJ. "I hope you don't mind if I work on cars in here. I ran it by David and he said he didn't care."

"What's ours is yours. You know that." She cast her gaze at Bob's newest collection. "You have your work cut out for you on this one. What is it?"

"Sixty-nine Plymouth Roadrunner." He grinned. "Beep-beep."

Bob's smile proved contagious. "That should keep you busy. How did you find it?"

Bob rubbed his shaved chin. "Nothing but luck. Alice and I went to an auto parts store in town and—"

"Alice Cummings? The president of ACU?"

He nodded. "The Chevelle needs a new radiator."

CJ sensed she might have opened the cover on the first chapter of a romance novel.

Bob squatted and looked down the car's side. "While we were at the store, a young man started talking to us about the Chevelle. The longer we talked, the more I realized the kid was a walking encyclopedia on muscle cars. It turns out he's a local boy and a freshman at the university. He knows every graveyard for old cars in this part of the state. He put me on to this one and went with us to look at it yesterday before dark."

CJ made a mental note of how "us" rolled off of his tongue. Her suspicions of something going on between her boss and her father-in-law grew.

Bob rattled on. "After some serious haggling, I made the deal."

He straightened himself and pried his gaze from the car that leaned to the left like it had one leg shorter than the rest. "I can tell you're not impressed."

"It's not that," said CJ. "I think this is a perfect hobby for you. I'm a little surprised Alice had time to go with you."

"Speaking of Alice, that's my first job."

"Huh?"

Bob threw back his shoulders. "You're looking at the CEO of The Bob Harper Male Escort Service. Alice is my only customer."

CJ shook her head. "I need to sit to hear this one."

They moved toward the barn's open door and retrieved two lawn chairs. Once settled CJ said, "Did I hear you say you're a male escort?"

He nodded. "Only one customer. Alice has a full calendar of social obligations, and going alone makes her a target for people who monopolize her time. She said she needs someone to run interference for her. You know, someone who can lead away the ones intent on a debate or looking for favors from her." The skin around his eyes crinkled as he smiled. "She figured an ex-con with a degree in mechanical engineering and who's coming into a small fortune would be savvy enough to keep away any self-absorbed erudite and those who'd had a drink too many."

He snapped his fingers. "And while you were sleeping, I received payment from the state for false incarceration. I'm now a millionaire."

CJ looked at the car with a missing back window. "You have an odd way of celebrating."

"We celebrated," he corrected. "Alice and I shared a banana split at the Dairy Queen."

"Now I know where David got his thrifty streak."

CJ placed her hands on her knees, leaned forward and rose from her chair. "What's the student's name that helped you find this hot rod?"

"Randy McNutt, Jr. I feel sorry for him. His dad's in prison."

The world around CJ closed in. Then it spun.

"Are you all right?"

"Uh... yeah. I just need to lie down again."

She made it as far as the kitchen sink. The chicken noodle soup didn't taste near as good coming up as it did going down. Did David know about his father's involvement with the young man responsible for her losing their child?

CHAPTER SEVENTEEN

Memories of a black car fleeing from campus police and her giving chase filled CJ's mind as she tried to rest. For the thousandth time she relived a pickup truck running a stop sign and clipping the rear of her patrol car. Images of her spinning out of control and slamming into a tree, the explosion of the air bag, and the surreal sense of loss replayed in a grainy black and white movie. The memory of searing pain, their unborn daughter leaving, and the screaming ambulance siren ripped at her heart.

A knock on the back door preceded a shouted, "Yoo-Hoo. Are you awake, CJ?"

Bea Stargate's voice drew her back to the present. CJ preferred to hole up in the dark bedroom alone, but of all people to visit, this was the best one she could think of.

The rustling sounds in the kitchen didn't last long. Bea's full head of blond hair and smiling face poked into the bedroom. "I thought you'd be up and at 'em by now."

CJ tried to speak but reached for another tissue instead. She wailed and crossed her hands over her abdomen, the last home of her lost child.

"Lord have mercy," said Bea in a soft voice. As was her custom, Bea didn't press for answers. Before she realized it, CJ found herself enfolded in Bea's embrace as her friend and confidant waited for the tears to subside.

Bea unwound her arms when CJ nodded and said, "I'm all right now."

It took one tissue to mop up the tears and two more before CJ could breathe through her nose. After taking in and releasing two deep breaths, CJ began her explanation. "It's awful, Bea. David's father is hanging around Randy McNutt, Jr."

Bea's expression didn't change. The placid countenance of peace covered the professor of psychology like a hand-sewn quilt.

At length Bea asked, "Does David know?"

CJ's response came out too quick. "I've been out of it for two days. We haven't said a dozen words to each other since Sloan died."

It must have been the tilt of CJ's head that caused Bea to ask, "What else is bothering you?"

CJ puffed out her cheeks to gain time to determine if she wanted to answer Bea's last question or not. One look into Bea's blue eyes convinced her to bare her soul. "Did you know David's dad and Alice Cummings are seeing each other?"

"Uh-huh."

"What about Bob starting a muscle car restoration business in the garage?"

"Yep."

"And him being a male escort to Alice?"

"Ain't it great?"

CJ flopped back on a pillow. "Am I the female version of Rip Van Winkle? I wake up and everything's changed."

"Change is the only thing we can count on in life," said Bea. "It's more fun if you ride the wave than fight against it."

CJ didn't have long to ponder the words.

"Billy Paul had lunch with David today. They talked about the car thefts and nothing else. I don't think David knows about the McNutt boy or Alice asking his dad to be her bodyguard."

"Bodyguard?"

"In a manner of speaking," said Bea. Without taking a breath, she asked. "How do you think David will respond to these things?"

CJ sat up. "He'll love Dad staying busy restoring muscle cars. It may take time for him to get used to Bob and Alice together. I had the same problem after my dad died. I resented Mom for wanting to get on with her life."

"And Randy McNutt, Jr?"

CJ groaned and looked straight into Bea's questioning eyes. "I can't say. He's come a long way in trying to forgive the men responsible for killing his mother. As for young Mr. McNutt, that may take more time."

Bea stood. "What about you? How much time will it take you to forgive him?"

CJ's stomach lurched as she looked up. "I love you to death, but you sure ask hard questions."

THE LAST SLIVER OF EVENING LIGHT PEEKED THROUGH THE living room window. CJ spent the afternoon in her favorite chair, staring out a window with an open Bible in her lap. She thought she'd worked through the grief caused by the accident, but, like an unpleasant habit, the pain returned. Despite repeating the mantra that she should forgive the irresponsible actions of a high school boy, the actual words of forgiveness had never reached the ears of Randy McNutt, Jr. The possibility of him interacting with David's father, being a frequent visitor to their barn, and possibly to their table, loomed on the horizon.

Bea's questions had hit home. How would David react? He wasn't one to sweep things under the carpet or pretend they didn't exist.

She sighed as she considered the talk they'd have when David came home.

To get her mind on something else, CJ retrieved her laptop to check her emails. Working her way through them, she deleted most and made quick responses to those requiring attention. The scrolling stopped as she caught sight of a new and unwelcome sender, Gloria Fishbaum. She opened the document addressed to Mr. Darden, Chairman of the Board of Regents. Copies went to all board members and Alice Cummings. The list ended with John Sylvester and Catherine Jo Harper.

Chairman and fellow board members:

This letter expresses my extreme displeasure with the actions and manner of a university employee in the last board meeting. The hostility shown by Assistant Chief of Police Catherine Jo Harper is inexcusable. It should be obvious to all that she is unapologetic in her use of violence and is training the officers under her tutelage and supervision to do the same. We should all fear for the safety of our university students.

The accounts of the actions she took prior to being hired by the university speak for themselves. I'm referring to her killing one man and maiming a second. You each heard the desire in her voice to repeat this form of back-road violence.

This leads me to question her mental state, and I find her inability to curtail the theft of vehicles from our campus to be unacceptable. Chief John Sylvester shares the blame, but that is a discussion best left for another day.

I demand Ms. Harper undergo a complete psychological and, if need be, a psychiatric evaluation. To avoid any hesitancy on your part because of cost, I'll donate whatever it takes to ensure we conduct these evaluations.

After the third reading of the email, CJ pulled down the screen on her computer. For the first time since she came to Agape Christian University she wondered if being a cop was worth it. She could stay home, farm their land, help at Billy Paul's ranch and raise children.

The back door slammed. David's footfalls signaled the approach of a husband who'd had a bad day. He sank onto the chair beside her and said, "Another car went missing from the university last night."

All thoughts of farming, ranching and raising children left her. "I'm going to work tomorrow."

He shook his head. "Too soon. You'll wind up back in bed."

She stood. "I'm going, and that's the end of this subject. But we need to talk. Bea brought something over this afternoon that Yari cooked. It's in the refrigerator. Get a bite to eat, then meet me in the bedroom when you're finished. I'll match you story for story on who had the worse day. It's time for me to take another one of those pills that knocks me out, so don't be long."

CHAPTER EIGHTEEN

A stack of papers awaited CJ on her first day back from the unanticipated time off. She plowed through the reports until the form of someone at her doorway caused her to raise her head.

"President Cummings," said CJ as she rounded the desk and received a hug.

Dressed in linen slacks, silk blouse and a light sweater draped over her shoulders, the president of ACU held CJ's hands as she asked, "Feeling better?"

"Hale and hearty. All I needed was massive doses of antibiotics and sleep."

"Good. Let's go."

CJ matched the buoyancy of her voice to Alice's. "Where are we going?"

The president's eyes sparkled. "I suppose your husband told you I joined him and that impressive Texas Ranger at the officers' shift change a few days ago?"

She nodded her response.

"It occurred to me, as I sat spellbound by their expertise and overall presence, I've never ridden in a police car. It's too lovely a morning to remain indoors. I've cleared my schedule for the next two hours. Let's go on patrol."

Not wanting to darken the mood, CJ avoided the scene of Chip Sloan's murder, now guarded by flowers, a menagerie of stuffed animals, and a white wooden cross. Despite the smile and enthusiasm, something in Alice's demeanor showed she wanted, or needed, to talk. CJ directed the patrol car to the deserted parking lot of the basketball arena where she stopped and turned off the motor.

"You're very perceptive, CJ. You knew something was on my mind. I owe you an apology. In my zeal to have you reach your full potential as a leader, I pushed you too hard. Before John came on board, the assignments and mentoring sessions I forced on you were excessive in the extreme."

CJ opened her mouth to speak, but a sideways glance told her not to. Alice had not yet unburdened herself.

"In addition, I ignored your personal life. You stood at the threshold of marriage and my selfishness could only see the needs of the university. Will you forgive me?"

"I forgave you before you asked." CJ paused and stared out the windshield. "I should have gone to the doctor with the sore throat before it waylaid me. If I'd paid closer attention to my time management, I wouldn't have put off my preparation for the board of regents either. I planned to be in bed at six that evening. As things turned out, I blew it at the board meeting and can't tell you one thing that happened at the sheriff's office."

A quizzical look passed over Alice's face. "You were brilliant at the board meeting."

"Gloria Fishbaum doesn't think so."

"Ah, Ms. Fishbaum, our resident contrarian. She argues an opposing point of view, even if she doesn't believe it. It keeps everyone on their toes and ensures we can defend the various positions we take." President Cummings once again looked full on at CJ. "You hated that meeting, didn't you?"

"Yes."

"Sitting behind a desk isn't for you either."

"It's not my favorite thing, but I realize it comes with the job."

"Yes, even jobs we love have responsibilities we don't care for." She shifted in her seat. "You heard Ms. Fishbaum's concern that enrollment will suffer if the thefts continued. The shooting and killing of an officer on campus makes enrollment concerns legitimate. Our recruiters and counselors are fielding questions concerning campus safety as we speak."

CJ had to nod in agreement. The best and brightest students didn't have to come to ACU. Their choices abounded.

"What are the other regents talking about doing to me? I know what Ms. Fishbaum wants." Something between anger and indignation welled up in her. "Are they going to put my name on the pink slip or John Sylvester's?"

"It's not that bad."

"That's not what I read in the email," snapped CJ.

A look of resignation crossed Alice Cummings' face. "After you left, the regents tabled a motion on a vote of no-confidence in John until the end of the semester." Alice added, "It's a threat without substance, a meaningless gesture of their frustration."

The car became claustrophobic. Moving to the back bumper, CJ lost herself in a cloud of anger. Who did Gloria Fishbaum think she was? She's nothing but a second-guesser, a Monday-morning quarterback, a fault-finder looking for scalps to hang on the wall of her upscale high-rise condo, or wherever she lived. She wouldn't know a proper police procedure if it jumped up and bit her on her skinny backside.

CJ lifted her gaze to the campus that rose in front of her. Compared to the boundaries of her previous job, this looked tiny—fifty-five acres versus the entire state. She replayed the voice of Captain Crow, offering her old job back to her. She imagined herself back in the familiar uniform of a state trooper, a uniform she'd dreamed of wearing ever since her father died. A uniform both had coveted. He'd always wanted to be a state trooper, but settled for being a deputy sheriff and farmer. She'd lived out the dream for both of them. Why did she throw that career away? If she returned, there would be no supervisory responsibilities and no need to coddle lawbreakers or self-absorbed professors. There would be no board of regents, and in particular, no Gloria Fishbaum. Going back would be easy.

She focused on the spire of the chapel. Minutes passed and her emotions stilled. A cool breeze blew across her face. The memory of Captain Crow's words faded. Gloria Fishbaum's face became a blur, replaced by a desire to grab herself by the scruff of her own neck and give it a good shake. The course of action came without fanfare.

Back in the car, CJ faced President Cummings. "In three days, I'll deliver a list of at least ten steps I'll be taking to make this campus the safest in the state. I intend on working here a long time with John Sylvester as the chief."

The radio crackled with the report of an officer reporting a traffic stop.

"Let's see what we can get into," said CJ.

"Yes. Let's do."

THE TRAFFIC STOP CONCLUDED BEFORE CJ AND ALICE arrived. Their patrol continued on to the edge of campus. Before them lay Highway 29, a major east-west highway that bisected Riverview and formed the southern border of ACU. CJ pointed to a bucket truck and a line worker attaching something to a telephone pole on the far side of the highway. "See that worker? That's some of David's diplomacy in action."

Alice's eyebrows lifted into a question.

"The Riverview chief of police got his feelings hurt when the Rangers took over the investigation. David got video cameras to cover every university street that empties onto city property. He told the chief he didn't trust me to put them in the proper places to catch the car thieves."

Alice stared at the workers. "Your betrothed plays the game of politics well." She squinted. "It looks like a bird house."

"The camera's inside, trained on the intersection. David knew it would draw attention if a camera hung at intersections that didn't have traffic lights."

"And the city will monitor them?" asked Alice.

"Not actively, that's not practical. The city puts them up and is making sure they're all in good working order. We'll tap into their data base and, hopefully, get a picture of a smiling car thief."

CJ pulled onto Highway 29.

"Was the chief of police pacified with placing the cameras?" asked Alice.

"David's slam on me pleased him more than anything."

"The things we do to soothe bruised egos."

CJ had her right blinker on when a car whipped around her and squealed onto one of the university's streets. Alice let out an audible gasp as the car came close to taking off CJ's front bumper.

Emergency lights activated, CJ grabbed the car's microphone and spoke in a voice trained to sound calm. "ACU 02."

"02," came the response from the monotone dispatcher.

"Show me out on traffic. Nora Victor Tom 1257.Highway 29 at Vista Drive."

"10-4."

CJ noticed her passenger had the look of a calf staring at a new gate, lost and confused. "I gave dispatch my location, the license plate of the vehicle, NVT-1257, and why I would be out of my vehicle. If anything happens and I need help, dispatch knows where to send them."

"This is exciting," said Alice. "Just like the movies."

"Open your door and stand behind it. Come to me when I motion so you can hear."

CJ approached the Honda Accord and waited for the window to roll down. The familiar face of the driver came as a surprise.

"Yari? What are you doing flying around me like that?"

CJ motioned to President Cummings, and she nodded.

"I'm sorry," blubbered the chef of The Campus Grind. "I'm late for work and..." Her left hand shielded her face and her shoulders lifted and fell over and over. Gasps for air accompanied sobs.

Yari's excessive reaction to being pulled over caused red flags to go up in CJ's mind. "When you calm down, get out your license and proof of insurance."

Yari raked tears away with her hand, smearing foundation and mascara. CJ moved forward to get a better look at Yari's face, but she continued to hide the left side as she pushed the documents through the open window.

"Step out of the car, Yari."

She complied.

"Move to the rear. I need to talk to you."

Head down, Yari moved to the rear as President Cummings back peddled.

"President Cummings, this is Yari. She's the chef at The College Grind." CJ did not attempt to pronounce the young woman's last name that bristled with consonants longing for vowel companionship. "Yari, this is Alice Cummings, President of ACU."

CJ turned to Alice. "I'll leave you two to get acquainted while I check a couple things. She returned to her car and raised the screen to her computer. She made checks for outstanding warrants. Periodically she glanced up to view the duo through her windshield. It came as no surprise when she observed Alice place her hand on Yari's shoulder in prayer. At length Yari nodded, CJ's cue to take care of business.

"The good news is you have no warrants and I'm only going to give you a warning. Don't interpret this as weakness on my part. If I see you driving like that again, I won't hesitate to write you a big, fat ticket. Do you understand?"

Yari nodded, eyes downcast.

"Look at me, Yari." CJ waited for Yari's head to lift. Pinks and reds surrounded a left eye, swollen almost shut.

"Did Speedy do this to you?"

"No." Yari's answer came much too fast.

"All you have to do is file a complaint and I'll have him arrested. I'll go with you to have a restraining order placed on him."

"No. You don't understand. He... he didn't do anything."

Anger rose in CJ. "The only person you're fooling is yourself. I've seen this more times than you would believe. It doesn't get better. It never gets better until you decide you can't live with it any longer."

"I can't."

The hesitating words, the denial, the downward stare of shame all added up to one thing. Yari was too frightened to act in her own best interest.

"Would you consider seeing a counselor?" asked Alice. "We'll pay you for any time off work. I can arrange it today."

"No." She looked at Alice. "Thank you. I'll be all right. I

need to get to work. I'm already late."

CJ exchanged a glance with Alice. She tore off Yari's copy of the warning and handed it to her. She didn't release the paper until she said, "I'll be coming to the bistro to check on you. Don't hide."

Yari turned to leave, but CJ caught her by the arm. "Go to a drug store and get an eye patch. Put on heavy makeup. It'll cut down on the questions and people staring at you."

Yari nodded and returned to her car.

Two seatbelts clicked. "I think I'd best get back to my office," said Alice. Then, as if checking off an item from a mental list, she asked, "Are funeral arrangements completed?"

"The day after tomorrow. They performed the autopsy yesterday, and the body is being transferred to Waco today. You should have the e-mail I sent to all university personnel with the details."

"Will most of your officers be attending?"

"I'm leaving a skeleton staff here."

"Such a needless tragedy," said Alice.

Upon arrival at the multi-storied Administration Building Alice asked, "Do you think the stealing of cars and trucks from campus will end soon?"

Her answer came without the least hesitation. "Before the end of the semester."

"What makes you so confident?"

"The murder of Chip Sloan changed everything. A coordinated effort between multiple agencies is underway. David's relieved of all other cases. His full attention is on getting to the bottom of this mess. We'll sort this out." She glanced at Alice. "Not convinced?"

"I'm no expert in police work."

Her pinched together eyebrows told CJ Alice had something on her mind.

"Go ahead, ask me," said CJ.

"I noticed at the shift change meeting when you were in the hospital that David had such a commanding presence. I've been wondering, why isn't he a Texas Ranger?" She paused, "If I'm intruding, please tell me and I'll not mention it again."

"It's because of his father."

Ever shrewd, Alice said, "I should have known. He's not a Ranger because if he sought the position, they might choose him. If chosen, the non-existent sins of the father would visit him by people who enjoy destroying others."

"Politics as usual," said CJ. "He won't accept it now, even if they offered. He's assigned to assist the Rangers. That means he stays out of the spotlight and we have all we could ask for now that his dad's exonerated and released from prison."

"Justice came much too slowly for your father-in-law."

"And it will come to this campus," said CJ with certainty. "Much more swiftly than it did for Bob. I'm sure of it."

Alice cocked her head. "You're convincing me. Keep it up."

CJ looked out the windshield as leaves scuttled across the street. "To allow David Harper to be a part of the murder investigation of a fellow officer is like putting a hungry blood-hound on the trail of a prison escapee dragging a thick steak." CJ paused. "Like David, I'm committed to putting an end to this. That's why I believe this case will soon end."

The university president reached for the door handle, stopped, and let out a cackle of a laugh.

"What is it?" asked CJ.

Still giggling, she said, "Oh, just a random thought."

"Tell me."

She opened the door, took a step back, raised a hand and in a voice suited for a Shakespearean play shouted, "Release the hounds!"

CHAPTER NINETEEN

A roll of her head did little to relieve the knot under CJ's right shoulder blade. She gripped the steering wheel even tighter as she passed a semi-trailer truck. "Do you want me to drive?" asked David.

"No. I want to get back to work."

David shot her a quick glance. "No need to snap at me."

CJ's gaze went to a faded American flag with a frayed edge whipping atop a rusty pole. "Lousy wind," she said. "You couldn't hear a word the preacher said."

"He wasn't a preacher. I don't think we missed much. He'd never met Sloan."

CJ cut her eyes to the right. "He didn't know Sloan?"

"He's a guy from the funeral home."

CJ kept her eyes on the road, her grip firm on the steering wheel. "I should have taken over the arrangements. Sloan's two boys deserved that much. All he got was a lousy graveside service from some guy who read a few pages out of a little black book. The way the wind whipped that puny excuse for a tent, you couldn't hear anything."

David shifted in his seat. "Lighten up. The arrangements weren't your responsibility."

"That's because Sloan's sister said she didn't want help. It looked to me like she tried to cut costs any way she could."

"Stop blaming yourself. If anyone's at fault, it's Chip Sloan."

She jerked her head to the right. Her hands followed, and the car made an unexpected lane change.

"Watch what you're doing," said David.

"Don't tell me how to drive." She righted the car, but not her emotions. "How can you say Sloan is to blame for his own crummy funeral?"

"Not the funeral, his life." David turned in his seat to face her. "The funeral reflected the kind of man he was. Sloan didn't plan or prepare. He made mistakes and didn't work to overcome them. Then, he blamed the consequences of his actions on others, including you. I've listened to you complain about him for months. Sloan was at ACU for eight years. Why didn't he take advantage of the free tuition? He could have prepared himself for a different career, something he was better suited for. He hated being a cop." David raised an index finger. "Answer me this—"

CJ held up a hand. "Enough!"

"Huh?"

"I said, 'Enough.' I don't want to hear any more about what a bad cop Chip Sloan was. In case you don't remember, he gave his life in the line of duty."

David stared out the passenger's window into a landscape that bent with the force of the wind. "No need to worry about that. I have a long memory when people are murdered."

CJ took the next exit and pulled onto a county road. She followed it until it dropped into the bed of a dry creek. Midway, on a low-water crossing, she stopped and put the car in park. Protected from the howling wind, she climbed out of the car and met David at the rear bumper. They didn't talk. Minutes passed before they wrapped themselves in each other's arms. She closed her eyes and allowed the rhythm of his breathing to bandage up wounds, old and new.

———

RESETTLED IN THE CAR AND IN THEIR RELATIONSHIP, CJ resumed their journey back to Riverview. "We're sitting down after supper tonight and you're going to look over the list of things I'm recommending to make the campus safe."

"Can do," said David.

"Any thoughts on the key in the Camaro?"

"Not yet."

The conversation came to an abrupt halt when the radio came alive with reports of a vehicle fleeing from campus. "That's Sergeant Ramirez," said CJ.

She sped up as David focused on radio traffic. Reports from assisting officers painted the picture. A truck from campus zig-zagged through Riverview. City Police units took the lead in the pursuit. Sheriff's officers were converging on Riverview, as were highway patrol officers.

"This may be our big break," said CJ.

She pegged the speedometer on ninety. Excited voices shouted from the speakers. The car stopped, and the occupants were held at gunpoint. Soon, the announcement came. They'd taken a pair of car thieves into custody.

When CJ and David arrived at the scene, the driveway of a single wide trailer, the connecting city street looked like a police convention with patrol cars sprinkled like confetti. CJ had to park behind a jumble of vehicles, many with their emergency lights flashing. She noticed a barn behind the trailer and pointed. David nodded but said nothing.

They strode to the epicenter of the action and examined the stolen vehicle. Shattered glass covered the driver's seat of the 2002 Dodge Dakota pickup. A long, flat, semi-rigid metal strip, three-feet long with a red handle, lay on the floorboard. A current student parking sticker clung to the back glass.

CJ followed David to the back door of a patrol car. He swung it open, and they peered at a pencil-thin, blue-jean clad young man wearing a black t-shirt. He looked at them through dilated pupils. A sparse beard, rotten teeth and fingernails stained yellow and black marked his appearance. An array of items including a wallet, keys, a crack pipe, a pack of Marlboro cigarettes and a lighter lay on the patrol car's trunk.

"Let's look in the barn," said CJ. They walked around the trailer and covered the twenty yards to the tin barn, a structure big enough for three vehicles. Only one filled the void, a twin to the stolen truck, except this maroon one had the hood up. The vehicle lacked many things, the most prominent being an engine.

On the way to CJ's car, they passed Chief Satterfield as he spoke to the second car thief.

The chief rose when he spotted them. A look of self-adulation flowed from his craggy face. "Looks like my boys got 'em. Like I thought. Local kids. There's no organized gangs in Riverview and this proves it."

CJ pursed her lips.

"Great work, Chief," said David. He extended a hand and gave an exaggerated shake. "We listened to the radio traffic as we came back in town. Your boys did a fine job. I can't tell you how glad we are that you cracked this case."

"Glad I could help you two out." The chief looked up at CJ. "I hope there are no hard feelings that I caught your thieves."

CJ bit her tongue, but forced a smile.

Their car door had no more shut when both of them burst into laughter. "When did you know?" asked CJ.

"The glass on the driver's seat was my first clue," said David. "What about you?"

"They had a Slim Jim to slide between the glass and door frame to pick the lock, but they didn't know how to use it." CJ couldn't control another string of giggles. "And the truck in the barn..."

David took up where she left off. "With its hood up, looking like a baby bird waiting for its mother to feed it a new engine. I doubt those two crack heads have enough brains to find a wrench, let alone swap out an engine. They didn't have an engine lift or a hoist."

"They'd give up, get some cans of spray paint, polka-dot the truck they stole and hope nobody noticed."

"If they didn't huff the spray paint first," added David.

Her laughter exploded again. She brought herself under enough control to say, "But the icing on the cake is that Chief Satterfield thinks he's solved the car thefts on campus."

"Doesn't explain the gang ink or the duplicate key does it?"

CJ placed her hand on David's forearm. "Have you ever noticed how laughter helps us deal with stress?"

"It's crazy, isn't it?"

Her hand found his. "I promised Alice we'd have the case wrapped up by the end of the semester."

David gave her a wink. "Then I guess we need to get busy."

"If you're half as motivated as me, we should have plenty of time. Let's go to campus and check with Sergeant Ramirez."

SGT. RAMIREZ'S PATROL CAR SAT IN FRONT OF THE UPD. CJ took an educated guess of where he might be and, sure enough, he occupied a seat in the break room, filling out a report.

"Excellent work on spotting the car thieves," said CJ.

The black caterpillar of a mustache had done an exceptional job of catching glaze from a demolished doughnut.

"Oh... *gracias.*"

"How did you catch them?" asked David.

Sergeant Ramirez preceded his explanation with a lackluster shrug. "Lucky, I guess. I parked down the road from the student union building. I noticed the window when they passed me. A good-size piece fell out on the road. By the time I turned around and called it in, they were leaving campus. I gave chase until two city units caught up with me. With so many cops responding, I broke off my pursuit and waited until they had them captured before I went to the trailer."

"You didn't stay at the scene long," said CJ. "We arrived ten minutes after they were in custody."

"Only long enough to get the license plate and the parking sticker number for my report." He pointed to the two-page form on the table before him. "They were going to impound the truck, and it wasn't my bust, so I came back to campus."

David stuck out his hand. "Good job. You're the one that first noticed them."

"No big deal. Right place, right time, I suppose." He returned to his doughnut and finished it.

"Drop that report off in my office when you leave," said CJ. "I'd like to go over it with David."

Once inside her office David said, "The chase didn't excite him much."

"He doesn't get excited about anything." CJ moved behind her desk and added, "Except doughnuts."

"Speaking of eating," said David. "There's stew in the freezer."

"How long will it take to heat?"

David grinned. "How long do you want it to take?"

CJ scratched her chin between her thumb and index finger. "At least forty-five minutes."

"I'll put it on low heat when we get home. Let's go."

"As much as I'd like to continue this conversation in a more meaningful way, we need to get down to business. If cars keep disappearing, we won't have to worry about scheduling our love life because I'll be on permanent vacation."

David sighed and picked up a pad from her desk. He wrote one word each on two separate pages: WHO, HOW.

CJ settled herself and retrieved her notebook. "Let's take who first."

"Our gang-banger cop-killer."

CJ nodded. "I think we can leave off the two druggies they hauled to jail today."

David cupped his chin in his left palm. "I know we buried him today, but put Sloan down with a question mark. You suspected him of being no good. Don't discount that gut instinct of yours."

"Sloan," she whispered. "He was a pain in the neck, and now he's a painful memory."

David continued, "Let's pretend for a moment that Sloan had something to do with stealing vehicles and his motivation wasn't money but revenge against you. Perhaps he knew someone who had connections with the Mexican Mafia that would do it as a favor. He'd been a cop a long time before coming to Riverview. He's bound to have rubbed against gang members in his past job."

CJ lifted her gaze from the list. "Have you checked his bank records? There may be a money connection."

"No unusual deposits, but they could've paid him in cash."

CJ looked down into the blackness of her coffee. "I'm having a hard time getting my mind off the key that Vargas used to get into and start the Camaro. How did he get a copy?"

David shrugged. "What about Maria Vasquez? I've heard you mention her name."

"Long shot," said CJ. "But she did grow up in a barrio of San Antonio. There's a lot of gang activity where she came from."

"Put her down," said David. "I worked my way through the alphabet with your other officers and found nothing of interest. I'll do a deep background check on Maria next."

CJ sat upright. "Do you think I might have another crooked officer?" Her coffee mug came down to the table in a thud.

"We're looking at all possibilities. What we know for sure is that we're still finding broken glass from the cars being stolen in the city and county. That stopped on campus, except for today."

"Showing keys are being used at the university," said CJ. "We're back to where we started. Who's getting the keys and how?"

David took a sip of coffee. "I'm convinced someone on campus is getting keys to vehicles and making copies of them. How can someone do that without the person being aware they don't have their keys?"

"I'll re-interview everyone that's had a car stolen on campus," said CJ. "I'll focus on the keys."

"Good. Now let's see that list of things you're proposing to make the campus safer."

CJ slid a typed list in front of him. "It's the usual stuff: more cameras, better lighting, educate for heightened aware-ness, develop relationships between officers and students. Also, I want to hire some criminal justice students as noncommissioned night foot-patrol officers. They can use their cell phones to call in suspicious activity." She paused. "I also want to encourage students who don't have a tracking device on their vehicles to purchase one."

David studied the list and said, "I like it. If we implement all these, it might be enough to scare them away from campus." Leaning back, he asked, "What are the chances of you getting enough money to do everything that's needed?"

CJ shrugged. "I'll send it to Alice tomorrow. Hopefully she can find enough money so it won't take board approval."

A silent pause in the conversation settled in as David reread the list of proposals.

"Honey," said CJ. "There's something else."

"Oh?" His gaze lifted from the paper. "I'm listening."

"It's about your dad and the Roadrunner he bought. It seems Randy McNutt, Jr. helped him find it and I'm afraid your dad will hire him to help with the restoration."

David rose, kissed her on the top of her head and said, "I already talked to Randy. He's not a bad kid, just a little lost. I think Dad's making Randy a project as much as the car."

"Do you mean to say you've forgiven him for what he did to us?"

"It wasn't easy."

CJ's pulse quickened. "And you're fine with your father welcoming him with open arms?"

"Randy took the Chevelle to work tonight while Dad puts a new starter in Randy's car. Dad trusts him, and that's good enough for me."

She managed to choke down a thought that wanted to escape her mouth. *You can trust him if you want. I don't.*

CHAPTER TWENTY

"Are you sure you're well enough?" asked CJ.

Chief John Sylvester eased into the black executive chair behind his desk. "It's good to be out of the house. A new wife and two daughters who can't decide if they love or hate each other didn't make for the most peaceful place to recover. Besides, I heard through the grapevine that my job is in jeopardy."

"I doubt that." CJ wished her words sounded more convincing. She lifted the pitch of her voice to sound upbeat. "When do you teach again?"

"Not until next semester. I'm on half-days until after Thanksgiving. It took every bit of my charm to get the doctor to agree to let me come back today."

John lowered his gaze. "I'm sorry I haven't been here to take some pressure off. Alice kept me informed of the grumblings from the board of regents."

"David thinks Ms. Fishbaum's goal is to get the new police building cancelled."

John tapped a pen on his desk calendar. "I hadn't thought

of that, but he's probably right. That makes me a pawn on the chessboard."

"Me too, unless we can put an end to the car thefts and stop the adverse publicity the school's been getting."

John shook his head. "Now it makes sense. It's just a game to her."

He put his palms flat on his desk. "The solution is simple, but difficult. Find out how they're getting keys."

"And who's behind it. We know it's the Mexican Mafia, but there has to be a connection here on campus or nearby."

"In the meantime," said John. "The stack of paper on my desk looks like three hours of work."

CJ rose. "It's good to have you back, boss."

He looked up with a smile. "Are you sure you want to work four hours each night slinking around the campus?"

"Maria and I will share the night shift. We're not telling anyone where we'll be."

CJ made it to the door before she remembered to mention something else. "It would be nice if the regents approved the funds for additional lighting and cameras."

John looked up. "If David's right, those items will be additional chess pieces. Now I know why the regents want me to attend their meeting next week. Even if we come away with our jobs, Ms. Fishbaum will trade two pawns and two knights for a queen."

The revelation of this being a game of politics hit CJ hard. Strategy and pre-determined moves were being considered, accepted, and discarded. Now she knew why she'd never liked chess.

<hr>

THE NOVEMBER EVENING SKY COMPETED WITH THE landscape to see which could outdo the other with fall colors of orange and burgundy. CJ made it home in time to enjoy some alone time on the back porch swing. While watching a pair of plump squirrels chase each other through the branches of a nearby pecan tree, David's SUV rounded the curve and parked under the carport. His early arrival buoyed her mood even more. He settled beside her and tilted back his Stetson.

"Good day?" she asked.

"A real good day. Burnett County officers nabbed one of the bad guys." He chuckled. "They didn't even have to work hard to do it. A rancher's daughter came home in the wee hours of the morning and caught a guy trying to hot wire her mother's car. The 30-30 she carried in her truck came in handy. It was unloaded, but he didn't know that. She kept him spread-eagle on their driveway for the twenty minutes it took officers to arrive."

"Was he a gang member?"

"Yep. Another prison rehab story gone wrong."

The pace and tenor of David's voice told her he had other news."

"Biff called me today."

"Ahh, that explains it. What did the class clown say?"

"We're having company for Thanksgiving."

ANOTHER RE-INTERVIEW THE NEXT DAY OF A STUDENT concluded with nothing of value gleaned. CJ stared at her desk calendar. With Thanksgiving break starting tomorrow, students will throw their dirty clothes in their cars and head home after their last class. Empty parking lots should mean a break in the car thefts.

Looking again at the calendar, she studied the red X on each day a vehicle was stolen from campus. Two weeks following Sloan's murder saw a respite from the dreaded red marks. The break proved temporary.

"Must have coffee." CJ spoke to herself, then reconsidered. "Coffee and one of Yari's chocolate figure-killers."

Bright sunshine, students scurrying, and images of cars being stolen resulted in an incongruent blend of contentment and frustration as CJ ambled toward the Student Union Building. Once again, the words of Captain Crow replayed in her mind. He told her she could come back to the highway patrol whenever she wanted. Yes, it could be a good life. She pondered the sentence and put the emphasis on the word 'could.' No guarantee.

The pealing of the chapel bell brought her stray thoughts back from their wanderings. She'd committed to put an end to the auto thefts, and she wasn't about to back out now.

She stepped off the sidewalk and moved under the canopy of one of the massive live oaks on campus. The trunk of the ancient tree provided a good place to pray. "Lord, I need your help. Please send someone or something that will help us solve these crimes. I love this place and these people. I want to stay on this campus. Thank you."

Once inside The Campus Grind, CJ's gaze fell on Yari. The chef grimaced as she struggled to carry a tray of scones and muffins.

"What happened this time?" asked CJ.

"Nothing."

CJ hands closed in anger. "That's the same lie as before. Broken ribs this time?"

Every breath Yari took brought a fresh grimace. "It's nothing. I fell."

"Whatever," said CJ with sarcasm dripping from the word. After a hard look she said, "My door is always open to you. When you're tired of being a punching bag, come see me."

Bea sat alone and motioned for CJ to join her. Once situated, CJ pulled out her phone and punched David's name.

"Do me a favor. Run a check on Yari's boyfriend, Speedy. He beat her up again and I think he broke some of her ribs... No, she won't file charges, but if something doesn't change... Yeah, okay. Thanks."

Bea patted her hand. "You're a wonderful woman. I've been sitting here watching Yari and praying someone would come along that could talk sense into that gal. I've tried everything I know, but I can't get through to her."

"While you're praying, pray I'll get a breakthrough on the stolen cars."

"Another one?" asked Bea.

"Not yet, but we have another problem." CJ glanced over each shoulder and leaned forward. "John met with the board of regents yesterday. It's just what we thought."

Bea nodded. "Billy Paul came in last night, mad as a wet cat. He wouldn't say much, but I knew where he'd been and assumed the meeting didn't go to his liking."

CJ lowered her voice to a whisper. "John looked shell-shocked this morning. The only thing he said confirmed David's hunch that the principal goal of you-know-who is to cancel the new building. I did some checking this morning and discovered the original vote for approval was split. It won't take much to make the board reconsider if enrollment projections continue to drop."

Bea let out a sigh. "That can't be all. I know my husband. He doesn't get upset about buildings and such. It's doing people wrong that makes him say words he shouldn't. Last night he used most of them."

Once again, anger swept over CJ. *Gloria Fishbaum wants to take all the pieces off the chess board in one fell swoop.*

CJ stood. "Desperate times call for action. I'm getting us each a double chocolate éclair."

Bea put on her most serious face. "I'm a firm believer chocolate has a way of putting life in perspective."

"Let's talk about Thanksgiving when I get back. Are you sure you don't mind having it at your place? There's going to be a mob."

Bea's face lit up. "You know me and Billy Paul. The more feet we have under our table, the happier we are." She pointed to the service area. "Get those éclairs and we'll get a jump on the holiday."

CHAPTER TWENTY-ONE

Looking out the front window, CJ caught sight of Biff and Amy's suburban as it topped the rise on the gravel road that led to their home. She spoke loud enough for David to hear from his office. "Company's coming."

He joined her at what her mother called the picture window and slipped an arm around her waist. "No peace and quiet for the next three days."

She leaned her head into his chest. "I never thought we'd fill up a five-bedroom home. All it takes is one visit from a high school buddy and his family."

"Bringing Nancy and little Davey makes it a full house, for sure."

CJ spun away from a hand inching upward. "Biff could use help to carry in luggage."

A windy carport served as the initial reunion site. Amy, the petite spitfire matriarch of the Stewart household, lined up the children as they piled out. The staircase of girl, boy, girl, boy, stated their names and thanked them for their hospitality.

Biff, with his ever-present toothy grin, bypassed David,

took CJ in his arms, and gave her a dancer's dip. "Did you miss me, honey?"

"I had a root canal," said CJ. "It reminded me of you."

Biff righted her, laughing. He went to David and embraced him in a long hug. "Good to see you, buddy. How's your dad?"

"As soon as we get you unloaded, we'll go to the barn and you can see for yourself."

Amy barked out an order. "Kids, get the luggage inside. Miss CJ will tell you where to put your things."

"Can we go play by the river?" asked the tallest in line.

"Not until after the meal."

"But, Mom."

A step forward and arms akimbo did the trick. All four broke formation and scurried to the rear of the suburban.

CJ thought she was prepared emotionally to have a baby in the house this weekend, but her breath caught when Nancy stepped out of the suburban holding a soiled disposable diaper in one hand and a squirming baby in the other. CJ and David had met Nancy earlier in the year when they went to Brazoria county for David's high school reunion. The trip turned out to be a life and death rescue for David's father, so they hadn't spent much time around the two of them. Now, there was no getting around it.

David took the lead. "It's only been two months, but I believe little Davey isn't so little." He turned to CJ. "Look how much he's grown. Why don't you take him so Nancy can gather up his things?"

CJ took a faltering step forward. She'd dreaded and longed for this moment. The question of how she'd react to the feel of a baby in her arms would remain unanswered as her offer of outstretched hands brought an immediate negative reaction from the six-month-old. He stiffened, turned, and buried his head in Nancy's chest.

"He's not used to driving for five hours," said Nancy.

Relief mingled with hurt. CJ sounded a chipper tone to cover her frayed emotions. "Let me take the diaper and I'll get rid of it for you. Don't worry about his bag. I'll get it."

In the meantime, Sandy came to investigate by sniffing. Her tail beat a fast rhythm as she received strokes from each of the children. She moved to Nancy and looked up. Little Davey reached out with a pudgy hand and giggled as Sandy gave it a three-lick greeting.

David and Biff took off to the barn, talking loud and laughing. CJ surmised Biff had delivered another of his patented jokes.

A black car eased to a stop, causing CJ's mood to darken. Up to now she'd been able to avoid Randy McNutt, Jr. Not today. When Bea learned Bob had hired him to help restore the Roadrunner, she issued an invitation for Randy to join them for the Thanksgiving feast. CJ had no choice but to share a meal with the person responsible for starting a chain of events that led to the loss of her daughter.

Lost in thought, CJ passed by Amy and the children, their ages ranging from seven to thirteen.

"Who's that parking by the barn?" asked Amy.

"Huh? Oh... yeah." CJ put a shine on her scuffed voice. "I'll tell you later."

"I need to pee," said the youngest.

A slap on the back of his head from an older brother caused the runt of the litter to squeal in protest.

Amy rolled her eyes. "Guess who he learned that from."

CJ led the way into the house and gave assignments. "Bedrooms and bathrooms are down the hall. Nancy and Davey, last room on the left with the twin bed and crib. Girls, you're next to Nancy. Boys, put your things in the first room on the right with cots. We haven't gotten around to furnishing that room yet."

She turned to the boys. "Sorry, pretend you're camping this Thanksgiving."

"Cool," said the head slapper.

Amy brought up the rear and deftly took care of last-minute squabbles, complaints and questions. The lone remaining room held a king bed and brought a firm nod from Amy. "This is perfect. Thanks so much for inviting us. The walls of our house were closing in."

CJ started to respond, but the door to Nancy's room quietly eased shut.

"Is she all right?" asked CJ.

Amy shook her head, walked toward the living room and whispered. "She's been sleeping on our couch for almost a month, with Davey on a pallet. Her mother's boyfriend tried to get friendly and Nancy dented his skull with a cast-iron skillet."

"Good for her," said CJ.

Amy's nod was one of partial agreement. "We love Nancy and Davey to death, but..."

A shout of anger preceded the slamming of a door. Amy scurried to the closed door and reached for the knob. "I don't know if I'm a mom or a referee."

It didn't take long before Amy joined CJ in the living room, staring out the window. No mention of the crisis or its resolution came from Amy. She cocked her head. "Are you all right? I'm sorry if we barged in on your Thanksgiving. Biff and I had quite a row about coming."

CJ looked down at Amy's small hand resting on her forearm. "I can't tell you how glad we are to have you here. Believe me, what's wrong has nothing to do with your visit. Having you and the kids and Nancy here is what I need."

Amy motioned with her head. "I noticed the swing on the back porch. Let's make a date for a long talk tonight."

CJ only had time to nod when the thud of shoes and Sandy's playful bark sounded from down the hallway.

"Can we go outside, Mom?"

"Yeah Mom. Can we?"

CJ rescued Amy from having to say no. "You'll have all day tomorrow to explore. Go to the barn and tell everyone it's time to go to Aunt Bea's. Ask Uncle David to let you ride in the bed of the truck."

A race to the back door ensued.

Amy hollered. "Don't slam..."

Bam!

"The door."

"Your bedroom has an en suite bathroom if you'd like to freshen up," said CJ. "We'll take our time and let the gang clear out."

"Is there time for a quick shower?"

"Take a long bath if you like. Billy Paul has instructions to keep the kids occupied for an hour."

Amy heaved out a deep breath and took quick steps to her room. "I've ascended to the third heaven."

CJ's thoughts turned to how she'd cope with sharing the Thanksgiving meal with Randy. She glanced at a calendar as she passed through the kitchen. If not for him, her daughter would have been born a week ago.

CHAPTER TWENTY-TWO

CJ smiled at the noise level of the dining room when she followed Bea in with the last of the side dishes. Fifteen pair of feet would be under Bea and Billy Paul's massive dining room table. It truly was a Thanksgiving feast.

Everyone settled in their chairs and joined hands while Billy Paul blessed the food and those gathered around the table. At 'Amen' the noise level came up like the volume on a stereo.

It didn't take long for the four rambunctious Stewart children to gobble down their food and ask to play outside. Biff waved them away, but Amy's permission came with a firm warning to stay far enough from the river to not get muddy.

CJ looked down at Sandy who, up to now, had mooched bites of smoked turkey from Billy Paul's plate. "Go with them, girl. Keep them safe." Eight feet and four paws hastened to the back door as Amy issued another warning. "If anyone goes in the pool, you'll all stay in your room until we leave."

The vibration of a cell phone caused CJ to look at David. He retrieved it, looked at the screen and rose. CJ knew the chances David would rejoin them with good news had a near-zero probability.

The small talk continued until he returned, sat and addressed the group. "Another stolen car last night. They took this one from a home in Cedar Park."

CJ exhaled an oversized breath. "At least it didn't come from ACU."

"I think it did," said David. "It's registered to the parents of an ACU student home for the holiday. A hooded man used a key to gain entry and drive away. A motion activated camera mounted on the home's garage captured the images of a guy wearing a mask."

CJ's chin rested on her chest. "And I thought we'd get a break over the holiday."

Little Davey added to the dark mood with a fussy whimper that threatened to break into a full-blown fit. Randy placed his napkin by his plate and stood. "Let me take him for a walk."

CJ winced as he held out his hands for Davey and the tike leapt into them. Why hadn't Davey done that to her?

Alice looked across the table at Nancy and said, "You have a beautiful child."

Nancy dipped her head, but didn't leave it there. She brought her gaze up and looked Alice in the eye. "He's a handful."

Biff broke in. "Tell President Cummings about your SAT scores."

Nancy's face turned almost as red as her hair. "I should have done better."

Biff didn't let it go. "I'd say being in the top five percentile in the nation isn't too shabby."

President Cummings' eyebrows shot up. "That's worthy of a celebration. What are you interested in studying when you go to college?"

She shrugged. "College isn't in my immediate plans. Miss Amy and Mr. Biff have helped me so much, but they have their own kids to raise. A job is my first priority. It isn't right that I'm sleeping on their couch."

Billy Paul spoke from the head of the table. "If you could rub a magic lantern, what would you like to be doing four or five years from now?"

"It would take seven years. I'd like to be a vet. Helping animals comes natural to me."

President Cummings looked at Biff. "How did she do in math and science?"

"Top two percentile nationwide. The social sciences brought her down."

Alice asked, "What's the most recent thing you've read related to veterinary medicine?"

Nancy didn't miss a beat. "A journal article on super-combo parasiticides. It's combining various drugs in a single shot or pill to give a broad spectrum of efficacy in treating parasites." Her head dipped again as if embarrassed. "I brought it with me and read it in the car."

President Cummings leaned forward. "It so happens some of our brightest scholarship students graduate next month. How would you like to move to Riverview and attend Agape Christian University?"

Nancy put her hand on her throat and then lowered it. "I checked the catalogue when I heard we were coming to Riverview. Besides never being able to afford it, you don't offer housing for someone like me. You know, an unwed mother."

"Books and tuition will be free," said Alice. "I can also get you part-time work on campus."

"I can use her with the cattle," said Billy Paul. "I need to hear more about those super-duper pills to make sure I'm not overpaying the vet."

"That still leaves you needing a place to live," said Bob, who up to now had sat silent beside Alice. "I'm willing to cover the cost of an apartment."

"No," said CJ.

Every person at the table cast their gaze at her.

"We have a five-bedroom house. Nancy and Davey can live with us."

When Nancy looked up, she beheld smiling faces. A stream of tears fell from each eye. Amy and Bea were on their feet and at her side before CJ could respond. She concluded there was a lot about parenting she needed to learn, in a hurry.

Randy reentered the room with Davey as everyone ferried dishes to the kitchen. "Where's Nancy? Did I miss anything?"

Bob slapped him on the back. "Nancy and Davey are moving here and Nancy's going to college."

CJ bristled. The thought of Randy influencing Nancy and little Davey made her question the snap decision. Also, she hadn't consulted David. What had she gotten herself into?

"It's not too late to back out," said Amy.

The porch swing creaked as CJ looked down the bank to the river and shook her head. She pulled a fleece throw tight against her. "I know the Lord told me to take in Nancy and Davey." She glanced to her right and chuckled. "It's the why I'm not sure of."

"The same reason He told me to. It's the right thing to do."

"I know, but I should have talked to David first."

Amy didn't disagree.

The swing kept up its slow, steady rocking. Amy let out a

moan of contentment. "I can't imagine a more peaceful place than this."

"Most of the time." said CJ. "We have our occasional brushes with reality."

Amy continued to stare in the river's direction. "I hear you're under a lot of pressure at work."

"I might lose my job and cause a good man to lose his, too."

"Biff said it's because of the car thefts. What else?"

CJ pulled a windblown lock of hair behind her ear. "I'm sure you heard about my officer being killed."

Amy nodded. "Such a shame. What else?"

"Isn't that enough?"

"It's enough, but it isn't everything."

"Are you talking about me and David not being in agreement about Nancy and Davey coming to live with us?"

"Who said you weren't in agreement?"

Even in the muted light, CJ could see the corners of Amy's mouth pull up. CJ thought for a few silent seconds. "Did David and Biff have this all planned out?"

"Not all of it. The free college and the job offer came as a pleasant surprise."

"David planned on us providing Nancy's room and board for the next four years?"

"He committed to it being a year and said it had to be your idea. He and Biff have been plotting for weeks."

More swinging in silence followed and served to dissipate a flash of anger. CJ broke the quiet when she asked, "How did we both get such good men?"

Amy shifted in her seat. "I don't know about you, but I'm still sanding off the rough edges from mine."

They both laughed in agreement and kept swinging.

A loud clang sounded from the garage. Both women turned their heads and listened for screams or something not fit for the children to hear. They turned back after laughter spilled out of the barn.

Amy faced the river and asked, "When are you going to forgive Randy?"

It might as well have been a knife in CJ's belly. She mumbled, "I'm trying, but every time I see him driving that car, my mind goes back to the night I lost her."

"It will affect your relationship with everyone in this house if you don't. Why do you think Davey didn't come to you? He can sense your anger."

The knife twisted. "Sometimes you're a little too direct, Amy."

She shrugged as she rose. "Bea told me that's how I needed to talk to you. I've delivered the message. Do with it what you will. You won't ever hear me say another word about it. I need to get the kids to bed."

"Wait, Amy. I'm sorry. I know you're right. It's just that I feel like I'm fighting against some evil force that's so much stronger than me."

"Do you mean within Randy?"

"No... well, maybe. I've never spoken to him."

"That's a good place to start."

***

DAVID TRIED TO SNUGGLE NEXT TO HER, BUT CJ EXTENDED an arm. "I understand I walked into your trap like a mouse to cheese."

He fluffed the pillows on his side of the bed. "It worked, didn't it? Besides, I don't hear you complaining about it."

She took a pillow from behind her head and gave him a light swat in the face. "Big dope. What if I hadn't spoken out?"

"Then Biff would have won our bet."

CJ pushed the pillow behind her and sat up straight. "You bet him I'd suggest we take in Nancy and Davey?"

"Yep. I figured my odds to be seven to one."

She reached for his hand. "I'm glad you won the bet. What odds do you give us on catching the car thieves before the semester ends?"

"Not good unless we catch a break. I've run backgrounds on everyone in your department and they all come up clean. I'm doubting it involves any of your officers. There's several with stretched budgets, but that's expected."

David moved closer.

"What do you make of the latest missing car in Cedar Park?" asked CJ.

"I studied the video before I came to bed. It was a slick job. There's no doubt they had a key. Because of the proximity to Austin, it wouldn't surprise me if there's a big chop shop somewhere in that area. I'm guessing on the east side of Austin."

CJ let out a sigh. "This car may mean Gloria Fishbaum wins the chess game. She's insisting on a board of regents meeting the day after classes are over. That's three weeks from now."

David scooted under the covers. "Let's get some sleep. We'll not solve anything tonight."

"One more thing," said CJ. "Any tips on how I'm supposed to start a conversation with Randy?"

David turned his back. "Just like tonight with Nancy. When the time is right, it will pour out of you and you won't be able to stop it."

She agreed with his words, sort of. Something would pour out of her, but would they be words to wound or forgive? There was only one way to find out.

CHAPTER TWENTY-THREE

Friday and Saturday passed in a blur. The Stewart children and Sandy explored every inch of riverbank and came home with mud caked from hair to foot. David and Biff spent most of their time with Bob and Randy, clanging and banging on the Plymouth Roadrunner. They managed to take a long break, retrieve shotguns and shoot clay disks on the far side of the barn. CJ and Amy took Davey to town to give Nancy some time to be alone and catch up on her reading... something about feline stomatitis. They didn't bother to ask.

CJ looked for the opportunity to speak with Randy, but an opportunity didn't present itself. Waiting wasn't her strong suit, even though she'd become better at it over the nine years it took for her and David to realize they needed to stop torturing each other and tie the knot. Both of them working as state troopers out of the same district office didn't invite a romantic relationship. Nonetheless, it came, in God's timing.

After lunch on Sunday, the Stewart clan, along with Nancy and Davey, loaded baggage and bodies into the suburban and expressed thankful goodbyes. Nancy would be back on

Tuesday if her 2004 Pontiac Sunbird had one more trip left in her. Bob gave her his cell phone number and promised to have the Chevelle gassed up and ready to come to her rescue.

Bob returned to the barn to continue work on the Road-runner with Randy. David went to his office to catch up on a weekend's worth of work. CJ looked around the house and considered giving it a good cleaning before she realized she was finding excuses for delaying something that needed to be done a long time ago. She slipped on a jacket and headed to the barn.

Conflicting voices carried on a conversation in her head. One told her she had the right to be angry. After all, the life of her daughter had been snatched from her by an irrespon-sible teen. He and his father had lied to avoid the conse-quences of his actions. He didn't deserve forgiveness.

The other voice didn't have its origin in her head. Instead, a series of passages from the Bible came into view. They were the yellow sticky notes she put on her bathroom mirror, each dealing with forgiveness. She'd read them for months.

She kept walking until she reached the barn. Hesitating at the door, she asked for wisdom and strength to be obedient, still unsure if she could. She shut out the other voice telling her she didn't have to do this and stepped forward.

Randy came through the opening, made a quick turn without looking, and careened into her. Gravity won the battle and she found herself looking up into horrified eyes. His hands reached for her, but then withdrew and raked his hair.

"I'm so sorry." He repeated the phrase three times.

She had no idea where it came from, but CJ couldn't help but smile. What started as a grin morphed into a guffaw and then into full-blown riotous laughter. It was as if the bottled emotions from months of grief and blame spewed out of her in a most unexpected way. There she lay, unable to do anything but laugh while Randy wrung his hands and continued to apologize.

She didn't know how long she stayed on the ground, nor did she care. She knew his apology went much deeper than an accidental collision outside the barn. After the last giggle, she extended her hand and Randy helped pull her upright. He continued to ask for forgiveness.

She brushed herself off and placed both hands on Randy's shoulders. "Listen carefully. I forgive you... for everything." She then pulled him into a hug.

Instead of words, he used tears to acknowledge he understood what she was saying.

CJ DRESSED FOR A NIGHT IN THE COLD. HER THOUGHTS shifted from Randy to students returning to their dorm rooms. The sprint to the semester's finish line would begin with Monday's eight o'clock classes. She refocused on the parking lots and protecting cars.

Arriving at the police department at 6:00 p.m. on Sunday, CJ attacked a pile of paperwork from the weekend. This early arrival allowed her plenty of time to finish before she started her half of the night shift. To her surprise, Maria showed up at nine thirty.

CJ gave her a quizzical look.

"I won't clock in until two. This is my first big case as a detective. I'll do whatever it takes, even if it means working more than you want me to."

"I know you're on salary since your promotion, but I can't ask you to work that many hours."

"Look at what I have at stake. Call it self-defense, if you want to. I don't want to break in two new bosses."

CJ made a steeple of her index fingers. "Why don't we

both work six-hour shifts on night patrol. I'll work the first six hours and you work from midnight until six and cut back on your daytime hours. We'll overlap when the most thefts take place."

"What about you working too much again?" asked Maria.

"John's coming back full time tomorrow. He'll take up my slack."

Maria gave a firm nod. "Sounds good."

Pointing to a box on CJ's desk, Maria asked. "Is that the Starchase?"

"That's it. The company sent it to John to examine. He's been meaning to send it back. There isn't room in the budget to equip the patrol cars with fancy tracking gadgets. They don't come cheap."

Maria picked up the box. "I watched a video on YouTube. These things can save lives."

"And catch bad guys. That's why we're going to mount it on my Tahoe."

A look of skepticism crept over Maria's face. "I'm not sure the company that sent it to John on approval would appreciate us sending it back used."

"They won't know if it's never deployed."

Maria grinned. "We can put it back in the box and if it's a little scratched, they'll think we did it handling it. Can we get it mounted now? I have some tools in the trunk of my car."

"Go for it. I'll be on foot. Call if you need me, and remember, cell phones only."

CJ's pony tail of long brown hair swung free as she set out from the police department. The night air had just enough bite that she realized December had displaced any chance of going without a jacket. She stayed in the shadows, changing locations and watching the late arrivals carry clean clothes and backpacks into the dorms. One by one, lights from the rooms blinked out, beginning around midnight. At 1:00 a.m. she watched Maria cruse by her hiding spot without seeing her. If the hyper-vigilant detective didn't notice her, no one else would.

CJ almost missed it because of the distance and darkness, but Maria had attached the Starchase. It reminded her of an undersized tube of tennis balls, about half the length and diameter. She pulled her phone from the pocket of her camo jacket and placed the call. "Pull over under a street light. I'm coming from behind you."

With motor running and lights on, Maria stepped out and left the driver's door open.

"Any problems?" asked CJ.

"The mounting was easy. Running the wire to the activation switch inside has me stumped. I looked at the instructions, but the page with lines and symbols meant nothing to me."

"I have an idea," said CJ. "I'll have my father-in-law check it out. We're finding it handy to have an engineer living in our fifth-wheel in the barn."

"He moved from the house?"

CJ spoke as she watched another late arrival unload. "He lasted two weeks; said we needed our privacy. I thought he might want to live somewhere besides the trailer after he received the big check from the state. He surprised us by asking if he could stay until he gets his restoration business up and making money." She paused. "I should have known. Bea said he'd be skittish about going out on his own for quite a while."

Maria went back on topic. "What about training for the dispatchers on the Starchase?"

"I'll talk to John about it when I come in tomorrow afternoon."

"This afternoon," said Maria. "It's Monday morning."

The two looked down at the device. Painted matte black, it blended in.

"Doesn't look like much," said Maria.

"Let's hope we have an opportunity to use it."

"I THOUGHT YOU WERE GETTING OFF AT TWO," SAID DAVID. "It's past four."

CJ rubbed sleepy eyes. "When your dad comes for breakfast, would you ask him to work on my Tahoe? Maria attached a Starchase to the push bar, but she didn't have a clue on how to wire it up."

"Where'd you get a Starchase?"

"John sweet-talked the company into sending us one on approval. The regents nixed equipping the entire fleet of patrol cars and approved the new building instead. He said he did it on purpose, giving them a minor victory so he could win the big one."

"Smart."

CJ raised a hand to cover a yawn. "What time do you expect Nancy and Davey to arrive?"

"It's a five to six-hour drive, so I don't think they'll make it until you've had a decent sleep."

After a brief detour to receive a kiss, CJ shuffled off to bed, hoping for many hours of peaceful rest.

CHAPTER TWENTY-FOUR

Nancy's baby-blue and bondo-grey Pontiac Sunbird arrived with a tail of blue smoke following. The brakes squealed the car to a shuddering stop in front of the barn. The engine continued to cough and sputter even after she turned it off. She restarted it, gunned the engine, and the motor gave a final rattle.

Removing herself from the porch swing, CJ went to lend a hand.

"I thought we'd never get here," said Nancy over Davey's screams. She wrangled her child from his car seat and continued her tale of woe. "He's hungry, tired, and dirtied his diaper forty miles south of Riverview. I was afraid if I stopped, the car wouldn't start again."

Randy appeared from CJ's blind side. "Let me take him. Hand me the diaper bag and I'll get him cleaned up."

Nancy handed him over and threw in a coy smile to boot.

"Where are you taking him?" asked CJ.

"Mr. Bob went to town while you were sleeping and bought a playpen and a changing table. It's in the barn by the trailer. He said Nancy and little Davey would be spending a lot of time with him." His head dipped. "Sorry, I should have asked your permission."

CJ stood stationary, not knowing how to respond.

Nancy took control. "Thanks, Randy. We'll get unloaded and fix him something to eat. I'll be out to get him as soon as I can."

By the time CJ recovered, Randy and Davey had rounded the corner of the barn. She turned to Nancy. "Let's get your things inside. There's a pot of stew if you're hungry."

"Starving, as usual."

Once inside, CJ put a lone suitcase on the bed as Nancy placed a backpack next to the crib.

"If you'll give me your keys, I'll get the rest of your things from the trunk," said CJ.

Nancy looked down. "There's nothing in the trunk but jumper cables. Momma didn't let me take anything when she kicked me out. Miss Amy gave me the suitcase and bought me enough clothes to get me by."

The confession took its toll on Nancy. She threw herself on the bed and buried her head in the pillow.

CJ knelt beside her, reached out a tentative hand and stroked a head of carrot-colored hair. "You're safe here, Nancy."

The tears subsided after a few minutes as Nancy righted her emotional ship as best she could. "I need to fix Davey his supper." She reached for the back pack and pulled out a box of dry cereal, and two jars of baby food. A can of powdered baby formula followed. "Can I use the kitchen?"

CJ took Nancy by her small, delicate hands. "This is your home. That includes the kitchen, the food, the washer and dryer and anything else you need."

"I... I've never lived in anything so big and nice."

"Neither have I."

CJ took a moment to consider her blessings and to issue a silent prayer of thanksgiving.

Instead of toting the meal to the barn, CJ called Bob and told him to bring Davey. She opened the door and viewed her father-in-law walking toward the house with the baby nestled in his arms. A moment later she saw Randy climb in Bob's Chevelle, crank it up and point it toward the gravel road leading to the front cattle guard of their property.

"Where's he going in your car?" CJ realized the question sounded like an accusation.

Bob responded first by bouncing Davey in his arms and making a clucking sound. When he came close enough he wouldn't have to raise his voice, he said, "I'm putting a new starter in Randy's car this evening. He's going to work."

"And you trust him with your car?"

Bob stopped in his tracks. "It's only a car."

"Only a car? That's your dream car. You said so."

"There are more important things than metal, plastic, and fabric." He bounced Davey in his arms. "Isn't that right, big fella?"

CJ blocked Bob's next step. "I'm sorry, Dad. I shouldn't have questioned your judgement."

Bob waved away the apology with his free hand. "I rigged up that fancy car tracker on your ride. You're ready to catch bad guys, if you can get close enough to deploy it."

"How close?"

"The closer the better. About the distance you could throw a rock left-handed."

"Thanks. I hope to put it to good use."

***

CJ joined John in his office late on Friday afternoon. He drew her attention to a large flat-screen monitor mounted on the wall and tapped his computer's keyboard. A map of central Texas counties appeared.

"I received this from David a few minutes ago," said John. "Every dot represents the location they stole a car from since January. Tell me what you see."

CJ studied the screen. "David mentioned this to me this morning. I was half asleep and didn't pay much attention." She stood close to the monitor and pointed. "The counties include all that touch Bexar County in the south to those that adjoin McLennan County in the north."

"Right," said John. "The heaviest concentration of dots follows I-35 from north of Waco to San Antonio." He rose and went to the screen. "Notice how many more dots there are around San Antonio."

CJ nodded. "Why do you think that is?"

John's eyes sparkled as he tapped on his keyboard and pulled up a spreadsheet. "David sent this, too. He must have finished it today. It's a breakdown of the auto thefts in each county starting in January. Tell me what stands out to you."

It was like being in John's classroom. A big proponent of the Socratic method of teaching, he required students to search out answers on their own.

CJ took a stab at answering her own question concerning the disproportionate number of red dots around San Antonio. "In the southern counties, vehicle thefts were steady from January until April when they spiked. They peaked in June and remain constant."

"Excellent," said John. "What about the counties farther north?"

CJ studied the spread sheet. "Nothing significant until August. Then, there's a steady rise until October. There's a slight decline for a week, but then it's high again."

John raked his hair with his hand. "Do you see it?"

"Uh... see what?"

He pointed. "David believes the Mexican Mafia set up a large chop shop in or around San Antonio last spring. They're using it as a prototype to develop similar shops throughout the state. Perhaps in other states as well."

"Holy smoke," said CJ. "Where's the second shop?"

"Most likely near Austin," said John, his voice now excited. "Look at the next page. It's an analysis of how the reporting cities and counties believe they stole the cars. Over eighty percent involved the officers finding broken glass at the scene."

"That's how ours started," said CJ. "We believe they broke a window, popped the ignition and drove away in the dead of night."

She turned back to the screen. "Are we the only ones with proof they used a key?"

"David isn't a hundred percent sure about that. He wants me to develop a program to cross check state vehicle registrations of all the stolen cars with the names of the entire student body, faculty and staff."

CJ spun to face him. "Why?"

"Because of the car theft in Cedar Park over Thanksgiving. He's trying to rule out if someone associated with the university is feeding information or keys to the gang."

"He's been a busy boy," said CJ. She looked again at the monitor. "What about the dip in October?"

John shrugged.

Then the answer hit CJ, and she moaned. "That's when they killed Sloan. They took a week off to let things cool down."

John went to the monitor. "You're right. Look, no stolen cars in or around Riverview for the week following Sloan's murder."

They stood in silence for about twenty seconds.

John turned back to his desk. "I'm surprised you didn't know about all this. Didn't David tell you?"

CJ took a step toward the door. "When I'm not sneaking around campus, I'm learning how to shove food in a dodging mouth or changing diapers. David's been on the road all week."

John pointed an accusing finger. "Don't you dare get sick again."

"Same to you." She spoke over her shoulder. "I'm going home for supper. See you tomorrow."

"Wait," said John. "There's something else we need to discuss. Close the door and have a seat."

CJ settled herself.

"This isn't easy to talk about, but I'm hearing rumors that a coup is being planned by some members of the board of regents."

"Are you referring to Ms. Fishbaum's plans to sack one or both of us?"

He nodded. "It seems her plans for conquest include me and you. If my sources are right, and I think they are, she wants to take down Alice Cummings, too."

CJ sprang to her feet. "Alice? Why? She's the backbone of this university and as fine a woman as you'd ever want to meet. She's dedicated her life to—"

John cut her off with a raised hand and a firm answer. "Ms. Fishbaum is questioning Alice's character."

CJ stopped in her tracks. "Her character? How could she question Alice's character?"

John pointed to the chair. "Sit down, lower your voice, and I'll tell you."

After plopping and crossing her arms, CJ nodded for John to continue.

He placed his palms flat on the desk. "My sources tell me there's been a steady drip of e-mails to the regents questioning Alice's relationship with your father-in-law. The words dating, convicted felon, ex-con, murderer and wife-killer are being bantered around."

CJ's hands were on John's desk before she knew she'd risen from the chair. "That woman's nothing but a cold-hearted witch. They framed Bob Harper and everyone knows it."

"Agreed," said John. "But its human nature for some people to believe the worst. Besides, this is about optics and positioning."

CJ threw up her hands. "You're talking politics again."

"Exactly. Ms. Fishbaum is trying to weaken Alice."

"Why?"

"She wants to have a greater say in board decisions and become the next chairperson of the board."

"And she doesn't care whose life she destroys in the process?" asked CJ.

"Apparently not."

CJ paced back and forth across the room three times. With jaw set, she sat back down in the chair. "What can we do to stop her?"

John shook his head. "Nothing comes to mind. Unless things change, Alice's influence will diminish and Ms. Fishbaum's star will rise."

CJ finished John's thought for him. "And she'll keep on until the black knight takes the queen."

"That's likely," said John.

"We have to stop her."

"Agreed, but it's going to take a Christmas miracle."

CHAPTER TWENTY-FIVE

CJ spewed invectives as Gloria Fishbaum's parrot-like visage taunted her on the drive home.

Upon arrival, she slammed the driver's door shut, took in a full breath of clean air and stopped to look around. This world looked and smelled so different from the stuffy office she'd left. Her anger quieted a little, but not her determination. Something had to change. It crossed her mind to pray more and think less. Easier said than done.

Nancy met her as she stepped through the back door. The almost-eighteen-year-old seemed to be dancing on the inside. She shifted Davey from one hip to the other, thrust her hand in her back pocket and pulled out a mobile phone.

"Look, Miss CJ. Look what Mr. David bought me. It's a new iPhone! Mr. David gave Randy a credit card and told him to take me to town and buy it."

Another wave of confusion came over CJ, but she didn't have time to distill it into coherent thoughts, let alone words.

"Grandpa Bob and Randy have been showing me how to use it. Isn't it the most wonderful thing you've ever seen?"

Grandpa Bob? Where did that come from?

CJ tried to respond, but Nancy cut her off. "That's not all. I already had someone call me. Guess who it was?"

All CJ could do was shrug before Nancy's words flowed again.

"Aunt Bea. Randy sent her a text on his phone as the salesperson was telling me about the features." She gasped for a breath. "Can you guess what else? Aunt Bea's taking me shopping tomorrow. She said it would be an early Christmas present."

CJ felt as if she'd been riding in a convertible at seventy miles an hour and had stood up. "Slow down, Nancy. You're going to blow a gasket."

That's all the rest Nancy needed. "Can you believe it? An iPhone, and it's the latest model. I've never owned a phone in my life."

"What?" CJ felt a wave of shame wash over her. *Who am I to be angry about those around her choosing to bless Nancy?* It was obvious she was the one with the problem, not Nancy.

Nancy's gaze went to the floor. "Mom wouldn't let me have one. She said all I'd do was use it to talk to boys. After I got pregnant, that settled the issue."

Bubbling over with renewed enthusiasm, Nancy proffered the phone to CJ. "Isn't it the most beautiful thing you've ever seen?"

For the first time in a while, CJ allowed herself to be caught up in someone else's joy. "Yes, it's nice, but remember, this is more than a phone. It's a symbol of your freedom. Use it and enjoy it, but don't take it for granted."

Nancy nodded and made eye contact. "Wow. You sound like a TV mom who always knows what to say to straighten out a wayward daughter."

CJ had no come back. All she knew to do was give Nancy

a hug. When they separated, Davey held his arms out for CJ to take him. She did, and he grabbed her nose and gave it a firm squeeze.

"Don't wear earrings," said Nancy. "I learned the hard way."

Nancy led the way to the kitchen. Davey spoke in baby jabber until CJ slipped him into a high chair, the latest addition to their dining table, where he banged his hands until Nancy produced broken pieces of graham crackers.

"I didn't notice Randy's car when I drove up," said CJ.

"Wash day. He said he's out of clean underwear. I hope he washes more than that."

"What did Mr. Bob do today?"

"Worked on the car and helped me find and download apps." She stabbed the face of the phone with an index finger and held it for CJ to see.

"What am I looking at?"

"That's where Grandpa Bob and Alice Cummings are."

CJ looked closer. "They're at Chez Moi?"

Nancy nodded. "Duck l'orange followed by a basketball game at the university. I told him it sounded incongruent. He laughed and said he needed to make up for sixteen years of beans, greens and cornbread."

"Speaking of food," said David as he came from his office. "There's left over fried chicken or frozen pizza. Take your pick."

"Pizza," said Nancy.

CJ gave him the obligatory peck on the cheek. "I hear you've been passing out gifts."

"It's the twenty-first century. If you recall, we don't have a landline."

CJ turned on the oven and stepped to retrieve pizza from the freezer. "Did you know your dad and Alice are having supper at Chez Moi?"

"Uh-huh. It's the same app I put on our phones."

"You loaded an app on my phone? Why didn't you tell me?"

He pulled back the refrigerator door and dragged out salad makings. "I thought I did. Didn't you notice it? You can track me, too."

Nancy spoke up. "You two talk a lot about tracking people. First it was that Starchase thing and now it's phones."

"Speaking of," said CJ as she looked at David. "We need to talk."

"Sounds serious."

"The queen is in danger."

"Huh?"

CJ'S MIND WHIRLED AROUND HER BOSS' DISCLOSURE concerning the plot to besmirch Bob and Alice, and her husband's reaction to the news. David sat expressionless as she relayed political intrigue. After long seconds of silence, all he said was, "John's right. That lawyer plays a mean game."

When she asked what they could do to stop Ms. Fishbaum, he offered no answer. Frustrated, she left David's office and returned to work, where she spent two unproductive hours staring at nothing but thinking about everything.

She started her shift a half hour early by parking on a hill overlooking the basketball arena and scanning the parking lot with binoculars. The distance to the near side of the sea of cars was only a hundred yards, but parking wrapped around the arena, only giving her a partial view of cars.

With her mind focused on intrigue, she didn't notice Bob's white Chevelle with wide black stripes running down the hood and trunk until it cleared the lot and turned away from her. She raised her binoculars and confirmed the sighting by the taillights and the last numbers on the license plate.

"They're going for pie and coffee," said CJ.

A half-hour later, people flowed from the stadium. The scene reminded her of disturbed ants storming out of their mound. Cars soon wormed their way out of the parking lot.

CJ's phone buzzed. David's photo shone on the screen. She swiped it and gave a terse salutation.

"Go to the basketball arena," said David with a serrated edge to his voice.

"I'm looking at it now."

"Do you see Dad and Alice?"

"No. What's wrong?"

"His car's not where they parked it."

Two unseen hands, one regret and the other shame, gripped CJ by the throat. She slammed her palm against the steering wheel. "I saw it leave. I thought they were going for a late-night snack."

"When?"

"Over a half-hour ago."

"Call it in. I'm on my way."

The phone made that annoying sound when it disconnects.

CJ reached for the microphone, but before she could remove it from its clip, John called dispatch and reported Bob's car as stolen. Then CJ remembered. John and Dotty were meeting Bob and Alice at the game.

Her chin fell on her chest. She saw Bob's car being stolen but wasn't thinking fast enough. "One step behind again," she whispered.

Bob offered a light-hearted joke that fell flat with everyone, including Alice. She hung on his arm and gazed down at the pavement with a look of dejection.

David's arrival did nothing but intensify CJ's regret. After mumbling a greeting to all those standing around a vacant parking space, he pulled CJ to the side.

"Did you get a look at them?"

CJ pointed past the stadium. "I was parked at least a quarter mile away on a ridge. The arena blocked my view of this spot. They made it to the entrance of the parking lot before I noticed it."

David's scowl left deep furrows in his cheeks. "Were other cars leaving?"

She shook her head.

He looked to the parking lot entrance several hundred yards away. "You didn't notice it when it came into view? What were you doing?"

"I... I don't know. Thinking, I guess."

He jerked his head to look past her. "Thinking? About what? It wasn't about people stealing cars."

CJ's slack posture stiffened. "At least I wasn't home watching television."

"No, you were out here thinking when you had a job to do."

"Back off," she said through gritted teeth. "I put the binoculars down for less than a minute."

"And that's all the time it took for Dad to lose his car."

She moved well within his personal space and looked up the three inches it took to make up for their height difference. "I said back off, Sergeant Harper. I'm on duty and I have a crime to investigate. If you're not here to help, I suggest you leave."

"You're right, I should leave. I'll take Dad home since he no longer has a car."

CJ strode to her car. Her eyes stung, but she made a vow she wouldn't allow anyone to see her cry. When she worked up the courage to look at the group again, she noticed David had left without his father.

Walking on unsteady legs, CJ went to where Bob and Alice stood. "It's my fault. I should have known something was wrong when I saw your car leave."

Alice closed her eyes and said nothing, which was worse than receiving a balling out.

Bob spoke up. "If it's all the same to you, CJ, I need to get Alice home. Would you mind taking her and then running me back to the barn?"

John spoke up. "Why don't Dotty and I take you both. We're in our mini-van. I don't think Bob wants to ride in the back seat of a cop car ever again."

"Good idea," said Alice. She looked at CJ and then at John. "We've had enough excitement for one evening. I want you two in my office tomorrow morning at 8:oo a.m."

Maria Vasquez drove up as John cleared the parking lot. She climbed out of her car and joined CJ as she stood in a deserted parking lot. "I heard," said Maria.

"Yeah, my father-in-law's dream car is on its way to being reduced to spare parts."

Maria said something in Spanish CJ didn't understand, nor did she want to. After long moments Maria said, "Go home. They won't hit again tonight. They never take three cars in a week. It's like they have a quota to fill."

CJ eyes opened wide. "Meet me in my office. I have some stats David worked up to show you."

Grabbing her cell phone, CJ typed in a text message to David.

Maria thinks the thefts on campus are part of a weekly quota system. Look at your stats for other areas and confirm.

She added,

And quit being such a jerk.

CHAPTER TWENTY-SIX

An hour later CJ tucked her SUV under the carport at their home. If failure had a face, she saw it in the rearview mirror.

David sat in his office with stacks of pages littering his desk. He looked up for a brief second. "Tell Maria there's a pattern. I haven't gotten it all figured out, but from what I see, the counties we're focusing on report the same number of vehicle thefts each week."

CJ moved behind him and massaged his shoulders. "What does that tell you?"

"Unless I'm mistaken, this is a sophisticated operation. More than ever, I'm convinced they're acting like a doctor's office where you need to book an appointment."

"Huh?"

"Okay, not a doctor's office. Let's say it's a high-end car dealership and you want to have routine maintenance done. You schedule a day and time. It maximizes efficiency."

The lightbulb went on in CJ's brain. "Same principle, except you never get your car back. By having a quota, the chop shops take in only the cars they can handle in a day."

David let out a moan of relief when she dug in with her thumbs. "Don't forget the neck while you're back there."

She moved her focus and continued rubbing. "Did you talk to your dad when he got home?"

David rolled his head. "He's borrowing your old truck tomorrow to go to car dealerships in Georgetown and Austin. He knows he wants a new SUV, but can't decide between a Lexus, BMW or a Mercedes."

CJ stopped rubbing. "Not another muscle car?"

"Both. The Roadrunner will be his new around-town toy. Whatever he gets tomorrow will be his work car."

"Work?"

"Don't you remember? He's the owner of Bob's Escort Service."

David reached over his shoulder and touched a spot on his right clavicle. "There's a knot the size of a walnut under there, dig deep."

He slumped onto the papers covering his desk as CJ concentrated her efforts on the knotty muscle.

"Right there, keep going."

"Honey," she said. "I may need you to help me with a couple of spots."

David turned to face his wife. "I think that could be arranged. But first, I need to apologize for being such a jerk tonight."

She leaned down and delivered a kiss. "I'm going to take a hot bath and forget about today and what Alice might say tomorrow morning. I'm looking for someone to scrub my back. Interested?"

"Very."

A random thought passed through CJ's mind when she turned to leave. "There wasn't any glass on the pavement where your dad parked his car. Do you think they had a key?"

He shook his head. "I don't see how, but I'll talk to him about it tomorrow."

CJ's eyes opened wide as a revelation hit her. Randy had borrowed Bob's car to go to work.

INSTEAD OF SITTING BEHIND HER DESK, ALICE JOINED CJ and John in chairs that formed a triangle. Bright eyes that shone with newfound determination replaced last night's downcast, defeated stare. Pleasantries weren't on the agenda.

"We're in a battle for our professional lives," said Alice. "I'm sure you appreciate the gravity of the situation so I won't belabor the point."

John asked, "Do you think it's that bad?"

"It's worse than I expected," said Alice. "Reporters from Austin, Houston, Dallas and San Antonio contacted me this morning, asking for interviews concerning last night's stolen car and my relationship with a certain ex-felon."

CJ couldn't respond. John put the pieces together. "Someone in Riverview tipped them off?"

"Yes," said Alice. "I have no proof, but I believe someone with inside connections here on campus is relaying information to one or more of the regents. The reporters know too many details. I could tell by their questions they'd been working on a story for some time."

CJ found her voice. "That's the sleaziest thing I've ever heard. Who do you think it is?"

Alice shrugged. "Someone with intimate knowledge of the university and the police department."

John looked at CJ. "That sounds like something Sloan would do, but he's been dead for weeks."

Alice shifted in her chair. "It won't do us any good to speculate. The best we can do today is damage control. I'm calling in a professional. It's her job to defend and not sound defensive."

She shifted her gaze to John. "I called Dotty while you were on your way this morning. I explained the situation and hired her as the university's public relations spokesperson. That's the same job she held for the state police and she's imminently qualified. I want you two and everyone in your department to refer all questions by reporters to Dotty. We can't stop leaks from anonymous sources, but Dotty can give the public a constant flow of truth."

Alice lowered her voice. "I won't sugar coat this. We may all be out of a job next semester." Her eyelids closed a fraction, giving her a look of determination. "I'm not without resources that our opponents don't know about." She rose and went to the window. "I'll not leave this campus without a fight."

John tipped his head to the side as a signal to leave.

He and CJ stopped at the base of the steps to the administration building. "How about a cup of coffee at The Grind?" asked CJ.

"I'd better call Dotty. Go on without me."

On this overcast day, CJ chose a different oak tree to stop under and pray. The prayer, however, remained the same. A request for divine intervention to bring light on the case came forth with renewed emphasis.

After a word of thanksgiving for the answers she hoped would soon come, CJ replayed the meeting as she walked. She felt both encouraged and worried. Alice, the diplomat, had never spoken in such a blunt manner. What were the resources she referred to?

Two things CJ knew for certain. Alice would not give up without one heck of a fight, and the car thefts had to end.

CHAPTER TWENTY-SEVEN

Yari stood behind the espresso machine mixing gourmet caffeinated drinks and trying to hide a split lip as best she could. Her head dipped when CJ tried to make eye contact. Instead of confronting her again, CJ ordered a raspberry scone, a tall coffee, and paid without a word.

Bea waved her over to where the mother hen of Agape Christian University held court. She'd caught Bea in between visits from students.

"You look like somebody ran over your cat," said Bea.

"Rough night to be a cop," said CJ.

"I heard somebody stole Bob's pride and joy."

"Bad news has wings."

"Same M.O?" asked Bea.

CJ nodded. "There's something clawing at my mind. There was no glass on the street. If someone used a key, how did they get it?" She became more animated. "And speaking of keys, I can't figure out how they made keys."

Bea shrugged. "It ain't hard to make a key. Take an original to any number of stores."

"I know that. But how are they getting the originals?"

Bea stood and opened her arms wide. "Brenda, my Lord, you're gettin' prettier every day. You're 'bout to graduate, aren't you?"

The girl, one of the many honeybees, smiled a crooked smile. A scar on her left cheek indicated a severed nerve that left one side of her face drooping.

"I have a job lined up."

"You don't say. What kind?"

"Plastics engineer. I start the week after graduation."

Bea's gaze shifted to CJ and back to Brenda. "Miss CJ and I were discussing something you might help us with. It's a head-scratcher. How would a person make a spare key if they didn't have the original to put on one of those key duplicator machines at a hardware or home improvement store?"

"Easy. Give me a key you want duplicated."

Bea scooped out a chain of keys from her purse and took one off.

Brenda looked at it. "This one won't work. Your car's too new and fancy. It's the chip in this that unlocks the car and allows the engine to start."

CJ slipped the key to her old truck off the ring. "Try this one."

"What make and year is it?"

"Ford, 1982." She looked on as Brenda placed the key on the table and used her cell phone to take photos from various angles.

"Next, I'd email these photos to my computer. You have to make sure the dimensions lined up, but that's easy. A 3D plastic printer goes to work and gives me a key that's identical to this one. It won't start the car because it isn't metal, but you can take the plastic key and make a metal one from it. Anyone with a small 3D plastic printer can do it."

"Why didn't I think of that?" exclaimed CJ. "Thank you

so much, Brenda. You'll never know how much. I gotta go, Bea."

CJ crashed through the door of the Student Union Building. She didn't realize she'd left her coffee on the table until she reached her office. Settled behind her desk, she whispered, "Now we're getting someplace. We know how, even if we don't know who."

CJ pulled out her phone and sent David a text.

lunch at hanks. big news

HANK'S B-B-Q JOINT MADE NO PRETENSE OF BEING A café, let alone a restaurant. It possessed all the attributes of a 'joint' in the truest sense of the vernacular. CJ entered through a squeaky door and took three steps down into a world that ceased to age sometime around 1970. Evaporative coolers, euphemistically called swamp boxes, protruded through wooden framed windows of the mid-twentieth century building. The coolers, not to be confused with air conditioners, served no purpose in winter other than to allow in cold air. Heavy plastic, secured by duct tape, covered them to keep out the most abusive drafts.

A bank of wood-fired cooking pits lined the back wall and provided the only source of heat to the building. Patrons could sweat, if they sat near the rear of the building, or keep their coats on if they chose a table near the front door.

CJ pulled a glass bottle of A&W root beer from a glass-front cooler and chose a table halfway between the pits and the door. She hummed along as a vintage Wurlitzer jukebox belted out Tammy Wynette's *Stand by Your Man*.

The door squeaked open again. David peeled off sunglasses and made his way to their table. "Ordered yet?"

"Waiting on you."

A mechanical cash register crowned the counter that had seen the better part of a century of commerce conducted without the aid of a credit/debit machine. A cherry-cheeked woman of forty-odd years asked, "What-cha havin', hon?"

"Brisket plate, and I'll get another root beer."

"Same for me," said David. "Except make it two bottles of Nehi Grape."

"Same price either way, hon."

Once back at their table they sat opposite each other. "Are we celebrating something?"

CJ nodded and leaned forward. "I know how they're making keys. They're taking photos of the keys and using a 3D printer to make a plastic key. After that, they—"

"Use a standard key duplicator. It's so simple, why didn't I think of it?" His gaze shifted to another group of patrons entering through the squeaky door and then back to his wife.

"There has to be a common thread that links all the keys together," said CJ. "Have you noticed anything in the reports I've been sending you? Do they all get their oil changed at the same place or use the same repair shop or car dealership?"

David shook his head and asked, "Are there any places on campus that require them to turn in their keys?"

She took a swig from the bottle before she answered. "I went back over every report this morning. The victims have very little in common, and they can each account for their keys. I'll send them a text and ask them to think harder. Somehow, somewhere, someone took a photo of each of their car keys."

A Styrofoam plate arrived with black-crusted sliced brisket, beans, and potato salad along with a quarter loaf of sliced white bread.

All talk of cars ceased. Sheets of paper towels off a full roll stood at the ready. David grabbed the bottle of extra-spicy barbecue sauce while CJ doused her brisket with regular. The melody of Charlie Pride encouraging the male patrons to 'kiss an angel good morning' took the place of conversation. It took CJ the entire song to quell her appetite enough to say, "I saw Yari again today with a fresh fat lip. What's the story on Speedy? Did you ever check him out?"

David had filled his mouth with bread and brisket dripping with sauce. He held up an index finger and chewed. After a long pull on the bottle of grape soda, he said, "No wants or warrants and no criminal history. I noticed something a little odd. Prior to eleven years ago, Mr. Beto 'Speedy' Gonzales didn't exist. I suspect he crossed the Rio Grande and kept out of trouble. He has a valid social security card and doesn't owe taxes. His financials checked out."

CJ stopped in mid-chew and stared at David with her eyebrows pushed together to register a question.

"Are you sure he doesn't have a criminal history?"

David continued. "None in the last eleven years under the name Beto or 'Speedy' Gonzales. No passport, nothing."

"Ah-hah," said CJ. "He assumed a new identity. And without fingerprints we can't find out who he is, or who he was prior to eleven years ago."

David looked up and grinned, "That sounds like a wonderful project for you this afternoon."

"Me? Why don't you do it?"

"I don't have an excuse to go see him."

The little upward tug on the right corner of his mouth meant he'd issued a challenge. "You scamp. You've been conniving a way for me to see that creep all morning, haven't you?"

"Something ran through my mind," he admitted. "I knew you'd want to get fingerprints on the guy who's been beating the tar out of Yari."

CJ accepted the challenge. "I'll get an excellent set of

prints from him and he won't know I did it. You can process them."

"Sounds fair to me." David went back to building another meat and bread half sandwich.

CJ pondered Speedy's new identity. Who was this guy?

"What are you doing this afternoon?" asked CJ.

"Checking on Maria Vasquez's bank records and spending habits, and waiting on you to bring me Speedy's fingerprints."

CHAPTER TWENTY-EIGHT

The Tahoe pulled through a gate that seemed more formidable than necessary. A ten-foot corrugated metal fence encased the graveyard for vehicles and mollified the sensibilities of those offended by the sight of rusting corpses of yesterday's must-have four-wheeled treasures. CJ passed a white car-hauler trailer backed up among the relics and stopped in front of a steel-ribbed metal building. Two roll up doors to the shop yawned open. Above a single door a sign read: SPEEDY'S. Glued to the door was a second sign that declared:

BEWARE, THIS PROPERTY GUARDED BY
HUNGRY DOGS, ONE NAMED SMITH AND
THE OTHER WESSON.

A dual threat of dogs and guns made CJ wonder if either were true. A firm knock put the first question to rest. Something slammed against the door and erupted in a riot of vicious barks. A harsh command quelled the dogs.

CJ cracked open the door after hearing the command, "Come in."

"Is it safe?"

"Sure, come in."

CJ eased into a cluttered office warmed by a combination heater/air conditioner sticking out a window. Both pit bull-dogs growled deep and low with gazes locked and muscles tense. "Hi. I'm CJ Harper with Agape Christian University. You must be Speedy."

The man stood behind a utilitarian metal desk that appeared to be salvaged from an army surplus store. Raven slicked-back hair ended at the collar of a black sweatshirt boasting a photo of a Tejano singer she didn't recognize. A single tattooed teardrop fell from his left eye. Otherwise, his arms were clear of ink, and unlike Yari, he had no piercings. What he had were dark eyes that flashed with suspicion.

"What can I do for you?"

CJ plopped down in a gray metal-framed office chair. "It's not so much what you can do for me, but what I can do for you."

He seated himself and leaned back with arms folded across his chest.

CJ continued. "I was going through our records and noticed we don't have you listed as one of our preferred vendors for towing vehicles from campus." She breezed on, not giving him a chance to respond. "It's the policy of the university to have at least three companies we can call on to haul off illegally parked or broken-down vehicles."

While she rattled on, she took out the first page from a three-ring binder and thrust it over the desk. "This is what we pay. Sorry, I should have made you a copy. I can e-mail you one if you'd like."

He took hold of the page encased in a plastic sleeve and examined the numbers.

"This is close to what I charge, but I'm not interested." He handed the plastic sleeve across the desk. "I run a one-man operation. Between the interstate and the city of Riverview, I have all the business I can handle."

"More work than you can handle? Business must be fantastic. Do you know of any other wrecker drivers I might contact?"

He shrugged in a way that told her he couldn't care less.

She rose and issued a quick thank you. Once the door closed behind her, she pictured herself slapping handcuffs on Speedy, or whatever his true name was. She'd know his true identity soon enough.

PONDERING THE ENCOUNTER WITH SPEEDY FILLED MUCH OF CJ's afternoon. She looked at a stack of folders on her desk and sighed. What else had she missed? The fingerprints she'd delivered to David should help, but she couldn't shake the feeling she'd overlooked something.

An involuntary shiver brought her back from the land of daydreams into the reality that if she didn't solve the car thefts, she might be an unemployed Mrs. Harper and not Assistant Chief Harper. The ring of her cell phone put an exclamation mark on the need to focus.

"What did you find out?"

"Speedy's name is Eduardo Mendoza. He served three years on the Ferguson Unit. He's out of Bexar County and he's an old hand at stealing cars."

"Any gang affiliation?"

"I haven't gone that deep yet. Why don't you call your buddy in Huntsville and I'll check with the gang unit in San Antonio?"

"I'm on it."

AFTER NEGOTIATING A LABYRINTH OF PRE-RECORDED prompts, an actual person answered at the Institutional Division of the Texas Department of Criminal Justice, AKA the State Prison in Huntsville.

"Classification and Records, Dominguez."

"Sammy, CJ David here." She used her maiden name since she hadn't spoken with the prison official since she married.

The voice changed from impatience to something relaxed and jovial. In her mind's eye she saw a short, chubby man with volumes of unfinished work in front of him. He greeted her with the same enthusiasm he did every time they'd studied together in college some eleven years ago.

"How the heck are you? I can't tell you how many times I've thought of you. It looks like you got your name in the news again. That was your cop killed by one of our alumni, wasn't it?"

The pain of losing an officer under her supervision struck again, like a bandage being ripped off a not-yet-healed wound. "Yeah, that's why I called. We think an ex-con named Eduardo Mendoza might have had a hand in the officer's murder and a rash of car thefts in and around Riverview. He fell out of Bexar County about five years before you started at the prison and I went to the highway patrol academy. DPS and FBI records show he served three years for stealing cars."

"What do you need to know?"

"Two things. Is there anything in his records relating him to the Mexican Mafia or any other gang? Second, what was his disciplinary record in prison?"

"Give me fifteen minutes. I'll pull his permanent file." He paused. "Better make it thirty minutes. Things are crazy today."

How to fill a half hour? The answer came from the police

radio. The dispatcher was sending the shift sergeant to take a report on yet another missing car. CJ moaned. She grabbed her phone and typed in a text to David.

Come to ACU. Another missing car. Answers on Speedy coming soon.

CHAPTER TWENTY-NINE

CJ went to tell John that David was on his way when she noticed a female student standing at the dispatcher's window. The young woman spoke as the door closed behind David. "Ma'am, you got a minute?"

"It's Rene, isn't it?" asked CJ. The five-foot-four-inch girl wore a t-shirt emblazoned with a 1970 Plymouth Duster. The shirt's material stretched tight across her ample chest while the bottom hung limp around shapely hips.

"What brings you in?" asked CJ.

Before the girl could respond David approached them and said, "Nice car. You a Mopar girl?"

She pulled the shirt away from her by grabbing the bottom hem. "That's right." A trace of an accent made the short sentence sound like "Dat's right." She added, "This was my grandpa's car. He left it to my daddy. Me and Daddy did a ground-up restoration on it. I'm glad it was my mom's beat up Honda Civic they stole and not the Duster."

David stared at the young woman with a mop of blondish-red hair, tiny upturned nose and a round face dotted with freckles.

His entire face seemed to smile. "Where were you when I was in high school? A cute Cajun girl with a hot car. Does your Duster have the 318 or the 340?"

"340."

"The Gold Duster Package?"

"No, but all the original badging and—"

"Sorry to break in," said CJ, even though she wasn't sorry at all. "I was reviewing your file this morning, Rene. Did you remember something?"

"I got your text, and it jogged my memory. I forgot to mention a Kindle and a set of wrenches were in my trunk when they took it."

"Did you have any identifying markings on the wrenches?"

"Dad engraved my initials on each of them. RF. Rene Fonteneau."

"That's a smart thing to do," said David. "You can't imagine how little things like that help us crack cases."

"Are you a cop, too?" asked Rene.

"This is my husband, Sergeant Harper," said CJ. "He's a state trooper who's helping us with the car thefts."

"That's awesome," said Rene. Her green-eyed gaze rose to David's face and locked on it.

"Was there anything else?" asked CJ.

Rene did an eye-to-ankle scan of David. "I have a question... maybe for both of you." Her gaze shifted from David to CJ. "Is it normal for an officer to take your keys during a traffic stop? The cops have pulled me over plenty of times for speeding in my Duster. I always turn it off to let them know I won't do anything stupid, but no cop ever asked me for my keys."

David stiffened. "Are you saying an officer stopped you and took your keys from you?"

"That's right."

"Where and when?" asked David.

"Here. Here on campus, a couple of days before they took the Civic."

"Why did the officer stop you?" asked CJ.

"No reason, except maybe to check me out." She shrugged. "Most often, it happens in the summer when I'm driving my Duster. He didn't give me a ticket or anything."

"Do you remember which officer stopped you?"

"I didn't catch his name, but he was real flirty. I had on a low-cut knit top and he kept staring. You know how some guys are." She looked away and blurted out, "That's him. The guy in the picture." Rene swallowed hard. "Is that the cop that was killed?"

The stars aligned. Answers, like pieces of a jigsaw puzzle, slipped into place, but not all of them. CJ took a step toward Rene and lowered her voice. "Sergeant Harper and I need you to follow us to the interview room. We have more questions for you."

CJ knew John needed to hear the interview first hand. "Sergeant Harper, could you take Rene to the interview room while I get us each a bottle of water?"

Her pulse raced as she told John the news. He watched, listened, and recorded the interview from the other side of the glass.

With the interview complete, David rose and walked with Rene to the front door. CJ leaned back in her chair and stared at the ceiling until David returned and plopped down in a chair. John joined them.

"What do you think?" asked John to whoever wanted to answer.

"I'm still trying to process everything." CJ's gaze remained on the ceiling. "What about you two?"

"Here's what we know," said David. "Sloan got the key from Rene and took it to his car. He must have taken photos of it."

"It all adds up to Sloan being a dirty cop," said John. "Not only that, but he fancied himself a ladies' man. We received two complaints for him flirting that I know of. We need to re-interview everyone that had their cars stolen and make sure Sloan took their keys back to his car.

"But what about the cars stolen recently?" asked John. "There's been plenty since Sloan died."

CJ looked at David and didn't want to ask the next question. "Are you thinking what I'm thinking?"

"If you're thinking you have another dirty officer, then yes."

CJ settled her chin in the palms of her hands. "If Sloan was giving the keys to the Mexican Mafia, why did he stop the Camaro?"

"Let's not get bogged down with that," said John. "Concentrate on the car they stole last night. We have hours of video to review from the cameras the city hung."

John went to his office to make phone calls.

Back in her office, CJ gave David a full and thorough kiss. Pulling away she retreated to her desk as if nothing had happened.

"Mind telling me what that was about?"

She fluttered her eyelashes. "You needed something to clear your mind of fast... cars."

"Ahh, that's it. A Duster-buster kiss." The smirk faded, replaced with mock seriousness. "Of all the muscle cars, that was my least favorite. It's a modified Plymouth Valiant, a little car with a 340 cubic-inch engine and fancy stripes that could get you into big trouble. It's built too squatty for my taste. I prefer something with a higher profile. More durable. Something built to last."

"Glad to hear it. You've got a reliable truck. Take good care of her and she'll last the rest of your life."

He flashed a roguish smile. "I love my truck."

It took everything she had to not give him a second helping. "You big flirt."

His smile came and went, replaced by an all-business gaze. "How many officers?"

"Three. I'm pulling one from patrol and two others will come in on their day off."

"You said the car reported stolen today was last seen at ten last night. That's seventeen hours of video times eleven cameras covering all the exits from the campus, divided by five of us to watch them equals to—"

"A big pot of coffee," said CJ. "I'll order out for something to eat as soon as everyone arrives."

David settled himself in a chair. "It won't be that bad. I'm guessing we'll finish by midnight. We can fast forward through the slow times and still be able to see a car as it comes into view of one of the birdhouse cameras. Get a blow-up photo of the car from the front view so we can refresh our memories of what we're looking for."

"I'll do it now." CJ did an internet search for photos of the make and model of the most recent missing car. "I hope we have better luck tonight than we've been having. Images of a hooded driver wearing a clown mask haven't done us any good. All we need is one clear shot and we can get help with facial recognition."

CJ ALTERNATED RUBBING HER NECK AND EYES AS HOUR after repetitive hour passed staring into a computer screen. Cars, trucks, delivery vans, motorcycles and bicycles came and went. The traffic decreased after 11 p.m., and she made use of the fast-forward button. A voice sounded from the office across the hall halfway through her third video. "Got it," shouted Lieutenant Page.

Footsteps converged on the room with two desks facing each other, both crowned with screens and keyboards. David squinted at the grainy photo of someone wearing a light-colored hoodie and oversized sunglasses. The car appeared identical to the one in the photo lying on the desk.

"The plates are right. That's our car," said David. "And that's our guy, but there's not much this photo will tell us tonight. I'll get this to some folks with special enhancing capabilities and facial recognition expertise."

Excitement waned as fast as it came. CJ thanked her officers and walked them to the door. When she returned, David sat staring and scowling at the screen. "I don't know what I was hoping for, but I didn't expect our guy to be wearing sunglasses at three in the morning."

She sidled next to her husband and gave him a one-armed hug. "Let me put some photo-quality paper in the copier and print the images. Maybe they'll be cleaner."

"I doubt it, but go ahead."

The copier made all the unique noises required and spit out three shiny photos of an unsmiling face behind the wheel of a stolen car. CJ went to her desk as David took a copy and studied it.

"It's better," he said. "But not good enough."

CJ pulled out a desk drawer and retrieved a magnifying glass, three times bigger than the largest she had ever seen.

"Where did you get that?"

CJ held it up to her face, making eyes, nose, and mouth look several times their normal size. "It's a gag gift I got for Maria Vasquez. I'm saving it for her birthday. Try to pick up anything else in the photo."

David put the photo on CJ's desk and moved the glass

close and then farther away. "Yeah," he said without raising his head. "There's something. Look at the guy's bottom lip."

She stood and used the same method to focus. After a few seconds she said, "You're right. It's a pierced bottom lip, and it looks odd." She refocused. "Did you inspect the sunglasses?"

"Why?"

Still looking through the magnifier, she said, "They're big and round. I've only seen women's sunglasses made like that."

"Are you sure?"

CJ stared long and hard and then lost her focus. She laid the glass on the photo and put her hand to her throat.

"What's wrong?" asked David.

CJ forced her gaze upward to meet his. "It's Yari."

CHAPTER THIRTY

Late the next morning CJ sat at her desk with eyes closed and hands clasped. A ring of her telephone brought her time in prayer to an abrupt end. She rose, squared her shoulders, and took the first step toward the reception area.

"Yari," said CJ. "Thanks for coming on such short notice."

Dressed in her chef's coat and black slacks, Yari added as much flair to her wardrobe as she could by wearing one pink and one green high-top canvas tennis shoe. "I was looking at something early this morning that I think you might help me with. Follow me and we'll talk in private."

Yari cast a furtive gaze and eked out an unconvincing, "Cool. Is this about my falling and hurting my ribs?"

"It's something else. Just a couple of loose ends I'm trying to tie up."

The room had a mirror on one wall, harsh fluorescent lights and three chairs. The first chair, a straight-back plastic model, had one metal front leg shorter than the other three. Although the chairs looked similar, the seat on the second chair measured an inch and half taller and scooted on plastic wheels. CJ motioned for Yari to take the short one. They faced each other, a comfortable three feet apart.

"How's everything at The Grind?" asked CJ.

"The semester's pretty much history. We'll have one last rush for finals, but it won't last."

"Any plans for a vacation over the Christmas break?"

"Yeah. I'm going to sun my buns in Cancun."

"Sounds awesome. I've never been there."

CJ rolled an inch or two closer. "Can I see your sunglasses?"

Yari's head cocked and her gaze telegraphed suspicion. "You said this wasn't about—"

"It's not. I know Speedy beat you up again, but that's between you and him."

"I don't understand. Why did you ask me to come in?"

"I'll get to that in a minute. I need an extra pair of sunglasses. I want to see how this style looks on me."

The glasses came off. Yari's eye exhibited a winter's day of colors: purple, blue, gray-green and yellow, all signs of recent and not-so-recent abuse. Her lip looked a little better, but the vertical line next to the silver loop piercing it still looked puffy.

CJ pretended to ignore the eye and the lip as she examined the glasses and tried them on. "What do you think? Do they work on me?"

Yari scrunched her nose. "Too bug-eyed. You look better in the wrap-arounds you always wear."

A text alert sounded on CJ's phone that confirmed her suspicions.

"Did you bring your car keys with you?" asked CJ.

"Yeah, they're in my purse."

"I need them."

Yari's head cocked to the left. "Why?"

CJ spoke in a calm, clear voice. "A police K-9 alerted us to drugs in your car. That gives us probable cause for a search. Officers are waiting for me to give them your keys." She increased the tempo and volume of her speech. "After that they'll tear your car apart, and believe me, they'll find every pipe, every rock, every roach, every stem and every gram of cocaine or whatever else you have." CJ extended her hand. "I'm not asking for your keys. I'm telling you. Hand them over."

Yari sat dumbstruck. A shaking hand reached into her purse and retrieved a wad of keys. An officer waited outside the door and exchanged the keys for a manila folder and a light gray hoodie. Opening the folder, CJ took out a photo but kept it face down on her knees.

She handed Yari the jacket. "Put this on. The sunglasses, too."

"You're scaring me. Why are you being so mean?" She donned the garment.

CJ raised the photo so only she saw it and alternated gazing at the photo and then at Yari. After several cycles, she heaved a sigh. The photo, a blown-up version, captured only Yari's face in the stolen car. She turned it to Yari and watched her reaction.

"Explain why the face in this picture and your face are the same."

Yari averted her gaze. "Well, ah, uh..."

CJ allowed the photo to drop to the floor. She projected as much accusation into her voice as she could. "I'll tell you why. It's because the person in the photo is you and you're driving a stolen car."

Yari tried to move the chair back. It rocked upward and fell back in place. CJ rolled her chair forward and put her knees between Yari's. Deep in Yari's personal space, she whispered with intended malice, "You're up to your neck in trouble." CJ jerked the sunglasses from Yari's face and tossed them across the room. "Look at me!"

Yari's eyes looked like wet ping-pong balls. Her hands and chin quivered.

CJ scooted even closer. "His name was Sloan, Officer Charles Sloan. He once pummeled one of your worthless boyfriends after the creep broke your nose. Remember? It was ten years ago, and you were my next-door neighbor." CJ allowed long seconds to pass before she tore back into her. "Chip Sloan was a cop. My cop. By some coincidence, he and you both ended up here at ACU. Chip Sloan." The name hung in the air. "You served him coffee at The Grind. And now, Chip Sloan is dead and you're a car ride away from wearing prison-made clothes for the rest of your life."

Yari's words came out like the scream of a wounded animal. "I didn't know they would kill him."

CJ turned up her volume even louder. "The heck you didn't. You've always had a knack for picking losers, but this time you chose a real dog, didn't you? Beto 'Speedy' Gonzalez. That's not even his name."

Yari's eyes registered surprise. "What?"

"You heard me. Your man Speedy is an ex-con named Eduardo Mendoza. He served a three-year sentence on a prison farm outside of Huntsville and did it almost day for day. They never declared him an official gang member, but they had strong suspicions. He was quick with his fists in prison, just like he is with you."

Yari hung her head. "I can't believe he—"

"You'd better believe it," shouted CJ. "He's going down for good and the only question left is how far down you're going."

Yari's hands covered her eyes, as if their placement could blind her from the truth.

"Speedy is supplying you with drugs, isn't he?" CJ didn't

wait for a response to the question. "He's also supplying drugs to people in Riverview."

Yari nodded.

"And guns, too. Right?"

A second nod.

"He brings them back when he takes a car or truck out of Riverview, doesn't he?"

Yet another nod.

"Chip Sloan had to die. He knew too much. Speedy ordered him killed, didn't he?"

"I swear to God, I didn't know—"

CJ's voice exploded in anger. "Don't lie to me. Speedy gave Vargas a gun to kill Sloan, and you did nothing to stop it."

"No! I didn't know until later." She shook her head with a vengeance. "I overheard a phone call. He bragged about it, but that was afterward."

"Who was he talking to?"

Black streams of mascara ran down her face. "I don't know. Somebody local, I think."

"Why do you think it was someone local?"

"I handed Speedy his phone. The area code of the caller was local."

"And the name?"

She wiped her nose with the back of her hand and smeared it on her pants. "No name. Only a number."

"What did they say?"

"It was in Spanish. I only heard one side of the conversation. Something about a Tech 9. I asked him later what a Tech 9 was. He beat me with a radiator hose."

If desperation had a face, it belonged to Yari. "Believe me, I didn't know. I tried to leave him." She pointed to her eye and held the other hand over her ribs. "This is what they do to me when I try to leave."

"They?"

"Yes," shouted Yari. "They. Now do you understand why I can't leave?"

Yari bent over, rocked back and forth and shook like a leaf in a thirty-mile-an-hour wind.

"I'll give you time to get yourself together," said CJ. "We're not finished."

David met CJ in the hallway and they stepped into the room with the recording equipment.

"Good job," said John. "We should have plenty after one more round."

A headache scratched behind CJ's eyes. "I feel dirty. In so many ways, she's a naïve little girl."

"Little girl in an adult body," said David. "She played a game and lost."

His arms folded around her. CJ stayed cocooned a few moments, then stepped back and asked, "What did they find?"

John answered. "A baggie of weed and a little coke. Not much of either."

"That should make this easier." CJ looked up. "Time for good-cop, bad-cop?

David turned the doorknob. "Let's do it."

The door opened with a creak loud enough for Yari to bolt upward, eyes wide with fear. She settled herself back in the wobbly chair with her arms wrapped tight around her abdomen. David leaned against a wall, giving a passable impression of a buzzard looking at road kill.

"What happens now?" asked Yari.

"It's up to you," said David. "You have two choices. One is bad. The other's horrible."

"I want the bad."

David held up a hand. "Not before you hear the horrible. And not before I advise you of your rights. You're under arrest. You have the right to remain silent..." He ran sentences together, not giving Yari time to think.

"Do you understand your rights and do you wish to continue talking to us?"

Yari nodded.

"You have to speak up."

Yari gazed upward and croaked out a pitiful, "Yes."

"We're not allowed to promise you anything," said CJ. "But Sergeant Harper will give you two possible scenarios of what might happen."

David jumped in, "First, you might be charged with capital murder. If convicted, that's an automatic life sentence or death by lethal injection."

"Capital murder? I didn't kill anyone."

CJ spoke in a subdued manner, as if she were apologizing. "A cop was murdered. Texas doesn't have an accessory to murder law. Most likely the charge will be reduced, but we can't guarantee that. Either way, you're looking at big time. You can also be charged with auto theft, drug charges, and you could be turned over to the Feds on RICO charges."

"Who's RICO?"

"Organized crime."

"How much time could I get?"

David stepped to where Yari sat, leaned forward and placed his hands on his knees while issuing a hard stare. "However long you plan to live, add a few years if they stack the sentences. First you do the time for all the state charges. Then, if you're still alive, you go to a federal prison."

"I'll do anything to get out of doing life. What's the not-so-horrible choice?"

CJ's took her turn, but as the 'good cop.' "That depends on how truthful you are, and it's loaded with *ifs*."

The tears had stopped, replaced with beads of sweat on her top lip. "What do you mean?"

"*If* you tell everything you know, and *if* you don't lie, and *if* what you say leads to a bunch of arrests and convictions, and *if* you agree to testify, the District Attorney might be inclined to go easy on you."

"How easy?"

"It all depends on how truthful you are and what useful information you give us. At this point, anything less than life would be a bargain."

David took his turn. "You'd better have something good to offer."

Yari pointed to her purse. "I have the key to the next car. I'm supposed to take it tomorrow night."

"You're lying," said David. "They never take over two cars a week from campus."

Fear shot through Yari's face when David accused her of lying. "I'm telling the truth. Speedy needs to get ahead to meet his quota because of the Christmas break."

"Let's pretend you're telling the truth," said David. "Where are you supposed to take the car tomorrow night?"

"To Speedy's."

"Where does he take it?"

Yari looked up and shook her head. "I don't know."

David stood, paced and rubbed the back of his neck. "How long does it take Speedy to deliver a stolen car and return to Riverview?"

"Four to five hours, maybe a little longer."

CJ's heart took a leap. They were ahead of the game. She needed to contact the owner of the car and get them to agree to their car being taken. What if it were damaged or destroyed? Would the university be willing to reimburse the student? She needed to call President Cummings. No. John needed to do that.

David's next questions brought CJ back down to earth. "What kind of car?"

"White Toyota Camry."

"Where are you taking it from?"

"Athletic dorm parking lot."

"When?"

"Ten forty-five tomorrow tonight."

"Will Speedy drop you off?"

"No. Too many cameras on campus. He'll go to Giovani's Pizza and wait for me to pass by. That way he'll know if I'm being followed."

"Will you take it straight to his shop?"

"Yeah."

"What about your car?"

She shrugged. "It isn't unusual for me to leave my car on campus overnight. I get one of my baristas to run me home if I get too mellow."

"What do you mean?" asked CJ.

"Look in my purse." She pointed to it on the floor. "There's a bottle of Percodan. If I think Speedy's going to knock me around, I'll take a couple before I leave work. It's crazy. He beats me up and then gives me pain pills." She cast her gaze to CJ and then to David. "I don't drive if I'm high. I don't want to hurt nobody."

"Sit tight," said David. "We'll be back and go over everything again. Think of what else you have to offer to help yourself out of this mess."

CHAPTER THIRTY-ONE

"She beats anything I've ever seen," said David after he shut the door to where John stood looking through the glass.

A mixed sensation of pity and satisfaction swept over CJ. "I can't decide if I want to hug her or lock her up for her own protection."

"I want her to get probation if what she said is true," said John.

"That'll be my recommendation," said David.

John stepped toward the door. "I need to call Alice."

The door closed and CJ tented her hands on her hips. "I was going to recommend we ask for probation. Don't you tire of reading my mind?"

"It's a good mind. It goes with the rest of the package."

How he could shift from one topic to another with such speed amazed her. CJ shook off his last bit of flirting.

John returned. "Alice said to tell the student that owns the car we're prepared to purchase it for three times the appraised value."

Next, with the speaker on David's phone engaged, they

called Ranger Blake Cruz and informed him of the break-through. A buzz of anticipation built when Cruz said, "We need to get moving on this. You two take those recordings of your informant and whatever else you dug up on Speedy and get a warrant to put a tracking device on that car hauler. Keep Sheriff Gladstone in the loop. He'll need search warrants for Speedy's garage, but make sure the sheriff waits until the car arrives at its destination. I'll call the D.A. and let him know what's going on. I'll also make sure he knows we're looking for leniency for this Yari woman. He'll want to put a wire on her tonight."

"I figured as much," said CJ.

"I'll keep well back and track the trailer from Riverview," said David. "We think it's going to Austin."

"You and I will go together," said Blake. Then, something in his voice changed. "If it turns out the destination is in Austin, their SWAT team will handle it. We can go in after they clear out all the bad guys but not before."

David looked as if he needed to spit something distasteful out of his mouth. He settled for, "This sounds like politics to me."

CJ asked, "What about me?"

"Captain Crow said you'd be right with us if you were back as a state trooper."

Anger flashed like a strike of lightning. "Well, you can tell that old buzzard—"

David broke in, "Tell him CJ said she's sorry she won't be able to come, but she has cookies to bake for him."

CJ shouted, "Laced with strychnine."

"I DO LIKE THIS TRUCK YOU BOUGHT TO PULL THE TRAILER," said CJ as she and David exited the grocery store parking lot and pulled onto the access road to the interstate. The truck's supercharger kicked in and she took the first on-ramp. After a silent mile David asked, "What's on your mind?"

CJ checked her side mirror. "I'm missing something."

"What?"

"Something Yari said has been bothering me. It's the local area code from whoever called Speedy and they talked about the Tech 9. That's important."

David shifted to face her. "Here's what we believe to be true so far. First, Speedy is taking the stolen cars to Austin and coming back to Riverview with drugs and guns."

"Second," said CJ. "The business with the keys. They're being used on campus to steal cars, but there's no evidence they're being used in the city or county."

"Right," said David. "We also know Sloan took photos of keys from cars he stopped on campus."

CJ mulled over the three bits of information. "Someone else is still getting keys from students and making copies." She paused as acid dripped in her stomach. "Everything points to me having another dirty cop, but who?"

"There's something else," said David. "Whoever your bad cop is, they will most likely disappear once they hear about the raid in Austin."

CJ moaned. As usual, David had figured out the next step. She had only a few hours to discover the identity of her second bad cop and arrest him.

David must have read her mind. "The rash of stolen cars will end as soon as the raid in Austin takes place."

"That's not good enough," said CJ. "We'll get Speedy, but I want everyone involved. I hate loose ends."

"Like why they killed Sloan?" asked David.

"Yeah. Everything points to it being a setup, but why?"

"Sometimes the simple answer is the best. Sloan wanted a fresh start."

"Do you think his conscience got the best of him?"

"It's possible."

CJ glanced to her right. "He thought I'd roll over and play dead when he was so disrespectful to me. No one ever hated me like that."

David twisted in the passenger seat to face her. "We'll never know why he acted so stupid. People make all kinds of bad decisions. Let's say Sloan got caught up in making photos of keys. Who would he send the photos to?"

"Speedy?" CJ considered her answer and shook her head. It didn't seem right.

"We're back around to that local number. Find the phone with that number and I'll bet it belongs to your crooked cop."

"I'm guessing it was a throwaway phone," said CJ. The answer to the identity of the mystery person, the second bad cop, stood out of her reach. The raids in Austin and tomorrow's searches might glean the answer, but would it be too late?

David opened the package they purchased at the grocery store and emptied one of Yari's Percodan capsules onto two balls of ground sirloin. He added the contents of a second pill for good measure. "I'll find out soon enough how mellow this makes Speedy's dogs."

CJ turned onto a private gravel road, crested a hill and eased down the other side. The formidable metal fence surrounding Speedy's Garage and Towing gleamed in the waxing light of a not-yet-full moon.

CJ asked as she eased the truck to a stop. "How are you going to get in? That fence is ten feet tall."

"I'm not sure, but I noticed there's enough of a gap in the gate for me to give those two man-eaters a treat."

David slid out the passenger door and crunched his way to the front gate. Alerted by the sound of the truck stopping, the two pit bulls erupted as he drew close. He leaned against one side of the gate and a two-inch gap appeared at eye level. He wasted no time in throwing the two balls of spiked meat into the compound.

David climbed back in the truck and pointed. "Drop me off at the corner of the fence. You can park on the crest of the hill and see everything through binoculars."

After selecting a spot on the high lookout, minutes ticked by with only the sound of the wind to fill the air.

Ten minutes later, a truck approached the front gate. CJ adjusted the binoculars and watched Speedy unlock a pad lock. Although a long way off, the clickity-clack sound of a chain being yanked through metal reached her ears. Then, she spotted David as he crept out of the shadows and squatted behind the truck. A cloud blocked the moon, and she lost sight of him. She held her breath. If she couldn't see him, neither could Speedy, or at least that's what she prayed.

A motion activated security light flipped on when Speedy's truck came close to the building. Where was David?

She scanned the area and waited. Several minutes later she noticed movement off to the right, behind the rusting heap of a mini-van.

An hour passed. Had the plan gone awry? It shouldn't take this long for David to affix the tracking device on the trailer. Where did he go?

She lowered the binoculars for a moment. "I'm going to kill him. What does he think he's doing?"

The door to the building opened, and Speedy yelled to the dogs. They wobbled on unsure legs and went inside.

Without warning, the overhead light came on and the passenger's door flew open. David piled into the truck and pointed. "Let's go. The tracker is on the trailer."

"What took you so long?" asked CJ, still trying to get her heart out of her throat.

"Doing recon. I pushed a window open enough so I could

hear Speedy. He kept trying to call someone and I believe it was Yari."

"What makes you say that?"

"Some phrases in Spanish are gender specific."

"We'd better get to campus and turn her phone back on."

CHAPTER THIRTY-TWO

Yari sat on a barstool overlooking the kitchen in CJ and David's house. "This is cool, like a sleepover."

"Not exactly," said CJ. "Unless you've been to sleepovers that involved handcuffing you to the bed."

Yari let out a giggle. "There was that one time. His name was—"

CJ held up her hand. "I don't want to hear it."

David chuckled.

Yari looked up. "You want to play cards or watch TV or something?"

"No. I want you to text Speedy what I told you."

CJ turned on the phone and handed it to Yari. Her thumbs typed out,

Too messed up to drive home. Will sleep it off and be ready for tomorrow night.

The phone chimed.

Be clean tomorrow or pay the price.

"Do you want me to cook you something?" asked Yari after she turned the phone off and handed it to CJ.

"No," said CJ, but David talked over her. "That would be wonderful."

CJ shook her head. "You two figure it out. I'm taking a hot bath."

It had been a long day and CJ had thrown the rule book out the window by bringing Yari home to spend the night. There wasn't a cell, or even a cot, at the campus police station, and they couldn't risk her being booked into the county jail. The important thing was to keep her hidden until she could steal the white Camry and deliver it to Speedy's.

The jetted tub worked wonders for CJ's disposition as she eased down into water almost hot enough to cook a lobster. She soaked until she nodded off then rose from the water. The aroma of frying bacon lured her into the kitchen after she dried off, donned pajamas and put on a robe.

"You need to go to the grocery store," said Yari. "The best I could come up with is biscuits, bacon, *huevos rancheros,* gravy, juice and coffee."

David looked as if he'd won the lottery.

CJ had thirds on biscuits that might have floated off her plate if they hadn't been slathered with gravy. David ate an even half-dozen.

While doing the dishes, Yari asked, "How many years in prison?"

"Shh," said CJ. "Nancy might hear you."

David had retreated to his home office, leaving CJ alone to field the question.

CJ whispered, "I don't know what the D.A. will do and I don't want to get your hopes up by guessing wrong. I can tell you that David and I have already spoken to him. Everything depends on how good the information you gave us is. You'd better pray that white Camry you're taking tomorrow night results in full jail cells."

CJ outfitted Yari in sleep shorts and a football jersey. A length of chain stretched from the bed frame to chrome handcuffs that closed around the houseguest's right wrist.

"This won't be bad unless I have to tinkle," said Yari.

CJ stifled a yawn. "I'll be on the twin bed beside you."

Yari nodded off like she didn't have a care in the world while CJ began a night that didn't promise much sleep. So much depended on what happened with the white Camry. She thought of Gloria Fishbaum and how much she'd enjoy pressuring the board to fire her, John and Alice. CJ even pictured her scalp hanging on the attorney's office wall next to her diplomas.

She looked at Yari and whispered, "This better smoke out my dirty cop."

***

AFTER DIGGING A GRAIN OF SLEEP FROM HER EYE, CJ pushed up from the bed and looked to the bed across from hers. She found Yari in a full fetal position, clutching a pillow and sleeping like little Davey with a full belly.

Her phone read 8:30 a.m. CJ intended to sleep late, but not this late. She jumped when it came to life. "John?" CJ whispered so she wouldn't wake Yari. The smell of coffee lured her from the bedroom and she eased the door shut behind her.

"I'm calling to let you know I'll be here all day and there's no need for you to come in," said John. "President Cummings told me to come to her office."

Coffee gurgled and sputtered as it finished brewing. CJ stretched out a kink in her neck. "That doesn't sound good."

"Our friend, Gloria Fishbaum, wants to put coal in our Christmas stockings."

Before CJ could reply, Yari called out.

"Was that Aunt Bea?" asked John.

"Yari and I had a sleep-over last night," said CJ. "David's late-night escapades were a success. I'll tell you about it this afternoon."

"Are we close?"

CJ reached for a mug. "Tonight should be interesting."

CHAPTER THIRTY-THREE

"You're looking chipper," said CJ as she sat in John's office. His eyes shone bright, nothing like the man who almost died two months prior.

"I feel great, but I've lost so much muscle it'll take me the better part of a year before I can compete in another marathon." His gaze shifted to a family photo sitting on his desk. "Considering how close I came to meeting Jesus face-to-face, I have nothing to complain about."

CJ updated John on the latest developments, including David attaching a tracking device to Speedy's car hauler and Yari spending the night more-or-less chained to a bed.

His eyebrows went up. "We'll keep that little secret to ourselves."

With her breach of policy destined for silence, she pressed on. "The theft of the Camry will be tonight, and not in the early hours."

John interlaced his fingers behind his neck and leaned back in his executive chair. "I wonder why they're changing the routine?"

"Perhaps it's because the owner of the car is a basketball

player and he'll be playing out of town tonight and tomorrow night."

John righted himself. "I guess it doesn't matter."

Something didn't sound right about John's response. Avenging the death of Charles Sloan, salvaging the reputation of the university and multiple jobs were all on the line. Everything mattered. A deviation in the M.O. could signal something bigger... but what? She'd been asking herself that very question all day.

She slipped so deep into her thoughts she had to ask John to repeat what he said.

"Is Yari to stay here until she walks to the athletic dorm tonight?"

"That's the plan."

It didn't take long for the plan to unravel.

A ONE-NOTE PING SOUNDED IN CJ'S POCKET. AT FIRST, SHE didn't react to the unfamiliar tone, but then realized it came from Yari's cell phone. The text message read:

Be at the shop at 7.

"This must be from Speedy," said CJ. "He wants Yari to come to the shop at seven this evening."

John scratched his chin. "Is this out of the ordinary?"

"Let's find out."

Yari looked up as CJ and her boss opened the door to the interview room. "This is nine kinds of boring. Can I get my phone back and play some games?"

CJ already had Yari's phone cupped in her hand. She held it out for Yari to read, but not take.

"What's this about?" asked CJ.

Yari's eyelids parted, and she raked her bottom lip with her top teeth. "It's bad."

"What do you mean?"

"No emoji. If he's in a good mood, he ends his text with an emoji."

John spoke up. "Does this mean a change in plans for you stealing the car tonight?"

Yari swallowed hard. "You're thinking about the car, but I'm worried about another broken rib or worse."

"You don't have any idea why he wants you to come, and why at seven?" asked CJ.

Yari's green hair shook from side to side.

CJ scrolled through Yari's texts to get a feel for how she communicated with Speedy and then handed her the phone. "Text him back that you'll be there on time. End it the way you usually do. Don't send it before I look at it."

Yari did as instructed, extended the phone to CJ and looked down.

Crimson rose in CJ's face, but she kept quiet.

"Isn't there a TV in this place?" asked Yari.

"Take her home and rest up for tonight," said John. "Leaving her in here any longer will cause suspicion."

CJ turned to Yari. "We'll leave in a few minutes." She followed John into the hallway.

"Did I see you turn red when you read her text?" asked John.

"I'm no prude, but that was the most X-rated ending to a text I've ever seen."

CJ opened it for him to see. He tilted his head like a confused puppy. "It's in Spanish."

"That's why I'm showing it to you. I knew you couldn't read it." She cast her gaze out a window as rusty December leaves cartwheeled their way to the ground. "I'm concerned about Yari. Do you think it's wise to allow her to go to Speedy's this evening?"

"You tell me," said John. "You know her and the situation better than anyone."

Despite not having a headache, she rubbed her temples with the middle fingers of each hand. "I think there's a good chance he'll rough her up again, but I don't think he'll kill her." She looked out the window again. "Besides, if we have an officer that's responsible for Sloan's death, I want him... or her."

John folded his hands in front of him. "Ask David and Blake Cruz. I've never been involved in a situation like this."

"You're looking tired," said CJ. "Perhaps it's you who needs to go home."

"No way!" He must have realized his response came out too strong. "Sorry. Nerves. I'll go home for supper and take a nap, but I'm coming back tonight."

"There's no need. It's going to be a nice easy car theft. David and Blake will follow Speedy to a chop shop. After that, it's up to David to convince Speedy to tell him who our dirty officer is."

"I hope you're right," said John. "There's so much riding on what happens tonight."

After retrieving Yari, CJ drove home and placed her in front of the television, where she took the remote and found the cooking channel. This time, CJ threaded the chain through the legs of a dining room chair, placed it by the couch and snugged handcuffs on her prisoner's wrists.

"This isn't necessary. We're ten miles from town and I know you trust me."

"I'm doing this for both of us. I'll write a long report after this is over. A slick attorney will try to tear apart both of our testimonies. That means I have to show I treated you like a suspect under arrest the entire time. You may not realize it, but my chaining you to this chair will give you one less thing to worry about." She pointed down the hall. "If you need to use the bathroom, take the chair with you."

CJ retreated to her bedroom, slipped off her slacks and blouse, and put on jeans and a red and black flannel shirt before calling David. The conversation didn't last long. She explained the text Yari received from Speedy and how she responded to it. The sigh of David's exasperation didn't surprise her, nor did his quick ending to the call.

A second conversation interrupted her nap in a recliner and didn't last long either.

"Blake took the information to Captain Crow," said David. "He wants you and some officers ready to go in if she needs help. He asked if you think you can handle it."

A jolt of frustration shot through CJ. "Does he think I'm a complete idiot? You can tell that buzzard-breath he can—"

David's laugh told her Captain Crow hadn't questioned her, rather it came from her husband's warped sense of humor. She tried to think of a retort, but he beat her to the punch.

"No time to discuss Captain Crow. I'll be on the same overlook we went to when I attached the tracker to the car-hauler."

Her phone went black.

Nearing the winter solstice, the afternoon sun soon slipped over the horizon and took the moderate temperature with it. Yari found enough left-over lunchmeats, Swiss cheese and bread to batter and fry Monte Cristo sandwiches. CJ moaned after wiping powdered sugar and strawberry jelly from her mouth.

"It's supposed to be dipped in currant jelly," said Yari.

"Any better and I couldn't stand it." CJ looked at Yari's plate. "You're not eating. Getting nervous?"

The answer didn't come for several seconds. "Why is it guys hit so hard?"

The bite of sandwich made a lump in CJ's throat. She chased it down with coffee. "Not all guys hit."

"That's easy for you to say."

"It can be easy for you, too."

Yari pushed her plate away. "Is this where you give me your God speech?"

"Do you want it?"

"No."

"Then I won't give it."

Green hair fell in front of Yari's face. She shielded her eyes with her hands. "I'm scared."

CJ knew she had to be firm with Yari, but not so firm as to alienate her. "This should scare you. You're where you are because of your own choices. I've known you for ten years and I've offered help again and again. President Cummings also offered to help you, but you turned her down, too. I bet if you tried, you could remember a hundred times when you had a choice to do what was right, but you chose not to."

Tears fell on the table. "It's too late. I'm going to get beat up tonight and then I'm going to prison."

CJ placed her hand on Yari's. "I'll not lie to you. You might get beat up and it's possible you'll go to prison. It's also possible that you won't. The real question you need to answer is, what kind of person do you want to be the rest of your life? A drug user? A man's punching bag?"

"I just want to have fun," said Yari between sobs.

"Are you having fun now?"

Her hair swung from side to side.

"Then do what you know is right. Choices and changes. Think about those two words."

The clock on the microwave flashed the time. "I need to

tape a wire on you. I'll be close and listening to everything. Tell me now if you want to back out."

Yari stood and took the plates to the sink. "That wouldn't be the right choice."

While taping the wire to Yari's skin at the top of her bra, CJ said. "If you feel you're in real danger, say, 'Please don't.' I'll be there in no time and arrest Speedy."

Yari looked up with determined eyes. "You won't hear me say that."

CHAPTER THIRTY-FOUR

A rock tumbled down the hill behind Maria. The undersized detective mumbled something low in Spanish, then switched to English. "It's so dark I can't see my hand in front of my face."

They topped the hill overlooking Speedy's garage, stopped, and squatted down. "Where's David?" asked Maria.

Before she could answer a hand went over Maria's mouth. A figure in black whispered in her ear. "Shh. You sounded like a lost cow coming up here." He released his hand.

In the softest of whispers CJ said, "I should have warned you. David was standing behind the cedar tree when we walked up. The Army's sniper school taught him all kinds of useful things. Concealment, stalking and stealth to name a few."

Maria turned to CJ. "How did you see him? He's wearing all black and a black ski mask."

"I closed my eyes tight for a full minute after I stepped out of the Tahoe."

"Why didn't you tell me to do the same?"

David responded for her. "This way you'll never forget."

"Darn right, I won't. Can you teach me concealment and stalking?"

David was answering when CJ interrupted. "Anything happening down at the garage?"

"Plenty. An hour ago, Speedy started a fire in a burn barrel. He also took boxes out of the garage and put them in the back seat of his truck. Twenty minutes ago, he ran to the gate and opened it. A decked-out 1969 El Camino SS came flying in and pulled in the garage. Ten minutes later he drove it in the car hauler."

It didn't take long for CJ to put the pieces together. "He's taking the El Camino to a chop shop and not the Camry from ACU."

"Not only that," said David. "The burning of what looked like files and transferring boxes to the truck means he's pulling up stakes. If we lose him tonight, we'll never see him again."

"Tell me about the El Camino," said Maria.

"It's sweet," said David. "SS 454 with all the chrome you could want. Black."

The corners of Maria's mouth lifted. "Speedy must have a grudge against Riverview's chief of police. That's his car."

"That's right," said CJ. "Chief Satterfield shows it off every year at the Christmas parade."

David had his binoculars up against his eyes. "Here comes Yari."

CJ turned to block the light from her phone as she checked the time. "She's late. Not good."

"Do you want to call it off?" asked David.

CJ chewed on her bottom lip. She weighed the pros and cons of rushing in to save Yari when she might not be in danger. The scale of justice tipped in favor of waiting. Her heart, however, told her to take Speedy down and not risk it. The final straw came when CJ remembered the look of determination in Yari's eyes and her commitment not to say the words that would bring help.

"She wants to go through with this," said CJ. "I'm going to let her."

David eased back before he stood. "I need to get to town and pick up Blake. Call if things change. I have three highway patrol units on back roads within three miles of here."

CJ brought her binoculars up and watched Yari go inside. She pushed the earbud deeper into her ear and listened as the shop's door slammed shut. No turning back. Yari had entered the lion's den.

"Where have you been?" shouted Speedy.

The snap of a fist striking flesh came through the earbud.

"Go start the car," said CJ in full voice.

Maria turned and scampered down the hill.

With binoculars still raised, CJ tried to get a glimpse of Yari through a dirty window, but the angle only allowed her to see a file cabinet with an open drawer. She focused on the conversation between Yari and Speedy.

"Why did you bust my lip again? Now I have to miss work tomorrow."

"Sit down and shut up."

"Why is the office such a mess? It looks like you're leaving."

"I told you to sit down and shut up."

CJ heard what she believed to be Yari sitting in a squeaky chair.

"Give me the key," said Speedy.

"Don't you want me to get the car tonight?"

A second whip-crack of a blow came.

"Here," said Yari. "Take it."

A few seconds passed and Yari spoke through tears. "Why are you handcuffing me to the chair?"

The urge to sprint down the hill and give Speedy some of

what he dished out to Yari almost won out, but CJ stood anchored in place, listening.

"Hey," said Yari. "You're taking my phone."

The sound of something crunching. CJ assumed it was Yari's cell phone under Speedy's boot.

His voice took on a less threatening tone. The volume increased, meaning he'd moved to within inches of the microphone. "We had some good times, that's the only reason I'm not putting a bullet in your head."

"But I love you. You can't leave me."

"I put padlocks on the outside of both doors. You can break the windows, but you can't get through the bars. Someone might find you in a few days."

CJ held her breath. Speedy would either come to the door or she'd hear a shot. Straining her eyes and ears, she whispered a prayer and waited.

MARIA HOPPED OUT OF THE TAHOE BEFORE IT CAME TO A stop at the gate. "He didn't lock it."

CJ shot the Tahoe through the gate as soon as Maria swung it wide enough. The SUV slid to a stop in front of the office door and CJ raced to dig a tire iron out of the back. The flat end slid between the hasp and the metal door. Pulling with all her might, the metal groaned but wouldn't give.

Maria arrived, but their combined strength wasn't enough to pop the hasp welded on a metal plate.

"Speedy didn't want her going anywhere," said Maria.

"Find a cheater bar," said CJ.

"Huh?"

"A piece of pipe. We don't have enough leverage."

Both scoured the graveyard of yesteryear's shiny new cars until Maria hollered. "I found something better."

CJ looked at the rusty tow chain with hooks on each end. "Perfect. I'll turn around. Hook one end on the padlock and the other on the trailer hitch. Leave a little slack, but not much."

The SUV shot forward. The door and hardware didn't stand a chance.

When CJ arrived, Maria knelt beside Yari, unfastening the handcuffs.

Blood dribbled from Yari's mouth; her bottom lip already swollen. She turned her head, spit, and looked at CJ with a narrow-eyed gaze of anger and resolve. "No man's going to hit me again. Ever. I swear it!"

CJ knelt and placed her hand on Yari's leg. "Do you need an ambulance?"

"No."

"We should at least take you to the hospital and get you checked out."

Yari flicked away the offer with her hand and then pointed at her mouth. "I've had a lot worse than this. Remember that guy in Waco? Now there's a man that could rattle your teeth."

After patting Yari's leg, CJ rose, took out her cell phone and pushed a name. The connection clicked on. "Are you tracking Speedy?"

"Yeah. How's Yari?" asked David.

"Her bottom lip looks like half of a hot dog, but she's fine. She gave nothing away. And I don't think she'll be looking for a boyfriend soon."

CJ took in enough air to ask her next question. "Is the tracker working?"

"Speedy stopped in town for a few seconds, but he's back on the interstate heading south."

"Hmmm," said CJ. "He stopped in town?"

"The truck stop on the south side. We've been staying at least a mile behind him." David paused. "Something's wrong. I could tell by your question."

CJ walked outside into crisp air. "Speedy took the key to the Camry."

The phone went silent for several seconds before David said, "You'd better get to campus and check on the Camry."

"That's what I was thinking."

"Don't use radio traffic or tell any of your people to check on the Camry. You may yet catch your dirty cop."

"I'm way ahead of you," said CJ.

CHAPTER THIRTY-FIVE

CJ eased the SUV to a stop. "I'll let you off here."

Maria unbuckled her seat belt. "Good thinking. There's nothing but open parking lots surrounding the athletic dorm. I need your binoculars." Trees and thick bushes made a line, three hundred yards from the Camry. She pointed. "I wish I could get closer."

"Will you be warm enough?"

Nodding, Maria pulled on a black ski cap. "Long underwear and two pair of socks."

After they'd driven to a street adjoining campus, Yari spoke from the back seat. "You're taking a chance."

"What do you mean?"

"Maria might be your dirty cop."

"She's not."

Yari leaned forward. "How can you be sure?"

CJ pulled over. "Ride up front."

The door handle slipped out of Yari's fingers. "You'd think I'd know by now that the back door on cop cars only opens from the outside."

The pair left campus and drove down empty city side

streets. "You asked about why I trust Maria. The previous chief was a good man, but he wasn't much on background checks for new employees. Things changed when I took over as the acting chief and Maria was my test case. I know more about her than I do my mother."

"Then how did Sloan get hired?"

"I inherited him. While I was working for the highway patrol, he was here."

CJ glanced to the right as Yari averted her gaze. "Still not convinced? Her credit rating is near eight hundred, and she saves twenty percent of her paycheck every month."

"Gangs deal in cash," countered Yari.

"True, but there's more. Maria doesn't brag. I've never known her to lie or even stretch the truth. She's humble. That makes her even more impressive."

"If you say so."

"There's one more reason I trust her tonight."

Yari turned to face her. "What's that?"

"Speedy passed the key to the Camry off as he was leaving town. If she were involved with the car thefts, she would've tried to call someone. She didn't and as far as she knew, I'd keep her with me all night."

"What if they don't take the car tonight?"

"I think they will. Speedy isn't coming back. He cleaned out the office and burned any incriminating evidence."

CJ swung the vehicle beside a convenience store's gas pump. "I'll top off the tank. You pick up some snacks and a cup of crushed ice for your lip."

"Then what?"

"We wait for a phone call from my husband, telling me Speedy is on his way to jail. We also find a nice quiet spot and drink coffee and munch snacks until we hear from Maria."

Yari covered her mouth with the back of her hand. "No

coffee. The stuff they serve here tastes awful. What time is it, anyway?"

"A little after midnight."

Another yawn came from Yari. "Why am I so tired?"

"You're coming down from an adrenaline rush. Take a nap in the back seat if you want to."

"Maybe later."

The Tahoe held seven gallons when the overflow preventer clicked off the flow. A second later CJ's cell phone alerted her to a message.

Warehouse in North Austin. SWAT going in now.

CJ nodded at the cryptic message from David, but relayed the information to Maria. She responded with,

Nothing to report.

The message CJ sent back read,

If no-show by 2, we trade places.

The clerk knew CJ by name, but raised her eyebrows when she saw Yari's puffy lip.

CJ moseyed down an aisle, staying close enough to watch and listen. Yari stood tall before the cashier and pointed to her face. "The guy that did this is being arrested."

Leaning forward, the clerk popped out a bridge of her front top teeth. "It cost my ex two years for each tooth." She raised her smock and showed the butt of a pink-handled pistol "I made a vow that I'd only go to the dentist for regular cleanings from then on."

The two exchanged a fist bump. Grinning, CJ filled a cup with ice and poured herself a cup of coffee.

Once outside, Yari asked, "Will David call when Speedy's arrested?"

"He's busy, but he'll let me know when he can."

The duo settled back in the Tahoe. "Where to now?" asked Yari.

"Campus. I'm scheduled to roam around tonight. It might tip them off if I don't make an appearance. We'll drive around and then I'll radio dispatch that I'm going home."

CJ's phone lit up with Maria's photo. "What's up?"

"Not sure," said Maria in a whisper. "A group of jocks are writing on the windows of a car close to the Camry."

"Are they causing any damage?"

"It doesn't look like it, but I'm far away."

CJ slowed to a more reasonable speed. "It's likely a prank or someone's getting married tomorrow."

"Do you want to clear them out?"

"What are they wearing?"

"Some of them are in shorts and tank tops. Others in hoodies."

"Stay where you are and I'll come talk to them. That should chase them inside."

A block from campus, Yari lowered the small amount of ice she poured into a plastic bag from her lip. "Still think they'll take the car tonight?"

The lights from all the electronics in the SUV gave Yari's green hair a spectral look. "I'd say the chances are sixty-forty in favor of it."

"Will they take it to Speedy's garage?"

"I don't think so, and that's what's bothering me. If I'm right, it means there's a second garage."

CHAPTER THIRTY-SIX

A group of seven young men trotted across the parking lot when CJ pulled into the athletic dorm's parking lot. As expected, white shoe polish spelled out a series of well-wishes for upcoming nuptials.

Fifteen minutes later, David's face appeared on her phone's screen along with a mechanical ring tone.

"Are you all right?" The words spilled from CJ.

"It went down without a hitch. They needed another sniper, so I watched from the roof until the building was secured. The chop shop's in a new warehouse district, one of those places with a business showroom in the front. A vast warehouse is in the back with loading docks and a ramp. They opened the ramp door for Speedy and SWAT rushed in before they could roll it down."

CJ tried to picture the warehouse. "Do you think there's another chop shop?"

"This one is big, but not big enough for the number of cars and trucks that are stolen each week. They built a separate room inside the warehouse that houses drugs, guns and explosives. We found RPG's, grenades, and mortars. ATF, FBI, and Homeland Security are here."

"Sounds like quite a party. Sorry I missed it."

"You could be here in less than two hours."

"Thanks for the offer, but I'm pulling an all-nighter."

She explained how Speedy's office looked, the burning of papers and Yari's treatment. The narrative ended with, "Speedy wasn't planning on coming back, and someone's going to take the white Camry tonight."

"I need to go," said David. "They're letting the press in and I don't want to see my name in the paper."

"Stay on the phone and walk outside. What did Speedy take with him?"

In her mind's eye she could see David walking fast and looking worried as he evaded reporters. Once clear of prying ears he'd fill her in.

"He had his personal items in the truck along with weapons, drugs and a laptop."

CJ thought out loud. "I hope they're dumb enough to take one more car."

"Are you watching the Camry?"

"Maria has first watch, but we'll trade places later. I'm creeping around campus with my lights out."

She looked to her left and noticed Yari's head leaning against the window with eyelids meeting in the middle. "My passenger's asleep. She had a rough night."

David's voice picked up. "Blake's walking my way. Got to go."

"You wore body armor, didn't you?"

"Full tactical gear. See you sometime this afternoon."

A patrol car sat parked in front of the liberal arts building. She pulled to a stop, got out and laid her hand on the hood. Cold. She gave a nod of satisfaction. The officer was patrolling on foot so they could see and hear better.

CJ stopped. Something wasn't right. Closing her eyes, she pictured her hand on the cold hood of a patrol car. She'd seen that image before, but when had she seen it and what did it mean?

She moved her hand to another spot on the hood. Why did it feel so cold? She closed her eyes and thought back to the night she'd crept in the shadows, looking for officers not doing their jobs. Maria Vasquez had stopped her and seemed offended by her slinking around campus. Chip Sloan was napping in his patrol car. A patrol car with a cold hood had parked on the street in front of the Liberal Arts Building in this same spot. She felt the car's hood again. "That's it." She ran to the passenger's door and jerked it open. "Wake up, Yari!"

THE MASTER KEY SLID INTO THE DOOR LOCK OF THE liberal arts building. CJ eased the door shut behind her and Yari. Shadows stretched long, and noise amplified in the empty hall.

Yari spoke through a yawn. "What are we looking for?"

"Shh. Something out of the ordinary."

They walked down a hallway. CJ tested the doors to offices, but not to classrooms. They entered a stairway and descended a flight of stairs. The rubber soles of Yari's tennis shoes squeaked on the polished floor.

"This is spooky down here," said Yari.

CJ nodded but said nothing. Her flashlight shone a white path before them as they trod on, Yari staying in step, shoulder to shoulder. Each door had a name plate beside it, except one at the end of the hall. The master key fit into the door knob but wouldn't unlock it.

"Why won't it open?" asked Yari.

"It's supposed to," said CJ.

A distant sound brought their gazes back down the hall as light bounced off the wall at the base of the stairs.

"University Police. Identify yourself!"

CJ breathed a sigh of relief. "Lieutenant Grimes, it's CJ. We're at the end of the hall."

"What's going on?" His flashlight shone on Yari's face. "What's she doing here?"

"She's in my custody," said CJ. She pointed her flashlight at the door. "What's in this room?"

"No idea."

CJ's flashlight shone on the knob. "Try your key. Mine won't open it."

The effort met with the same results. Lieutenant Grimes clipped his keys back on his belt. "Sgt. Ramirez always checks this building."

A sense of alarm swept over CJ. "Where's Sergeant Ramirez now?"

He shrugged. "His car's out front, so he must be on foot. I'll get him on the radio."

CJ looked past her lieutenant into darkness. "Stay off the radio. Go to your car and get a tire tool."

It seemed to take forever before the lieutenant sprinted back down the hall with tire tool in hand. He drove it into the gap above the door latch and pulled. Metal creaked. He took another bite, this time below the locking mechanism. Metal groaned again, but the door refused to open. One more thrust in the gap, one more grunt of effort, and the door sprung open. A flip of the switch and the room flooded with light.

Intended as a janitor's storage, the room looked like a makeshift dorm room with a cot nestled against one wall. It also contained a desk, chair, a small refrigerator and a coffee pot. CJ jerked a black cover from something the size of a microwave. Beneath it was a plastic duplicating machine. An empty box of doughnuts sat on the desk along with a blank note pad.

The lieutenant huffed in disgust. "So, this is where he spends his time. No wonder he takes so long to respond. He has to wake up."

CJ moved to the desk and picked up the pad. She turned it to where it caught the light. Retrieving a pencil from the drawer, she rubbed the side of the lead over the pad. Numbers and letters appeared as if by magic. T-C-WAD RVP-2498.

Yari looked around her shoulder. "What does that mean?"

"You should know," said CJ. "That was your score tonight. Toyota Camry. White. Athletic Dorm, and the license plate."

CJ's phone came alive. She didn't quite have it to her ear when Maria said, "The Camry's on the move. I didn't see the perp until the car started."

"Meet me on the street, Maria. I know who it is and where he's going."

CJ spun and ran out of the room. "Come on you two, we need to hurry."

The trio burst from the building and made for the street. CJ stopped at her car and turned to the lieutenant. "Cuff her. Stay off the radio and put her in the interview room. Call the chief, he'll know what to do with her."

Yari looked like a frightened child with eyes wide and questioning. CJ heard the ratcheting of the handcuffs. "You promised to help me," shouted Yari.

"I am. You're under arrest and I don't have time to talk about it now."

CHAPTER THIRTY-SEVEN

The Tahoe slid to a stop, and Maria piled into the front seat.

"When did he take the car?" asked CJ.

"Six minutes ago. What took you so long?"

"It's Sergeant Ramirez. He had a cozy setup in the basement of the liberal arts building—cot, refrigerator, key duplicator and snacks."

Maria's jaw ground back and forth.

CJ tapped her brakes before she slid the car sideways onto Highway 29 and sped into the heart of Riverview. "Ramirez lives on the northwest side of town. I know the subdivision, but not his address."

Maria took out her cell phone and manipulated it. "He'll take Woodland Park Drive to his house and back to the interstate."

CJ activated emergency lights, but not the siren. The town slumbered as they blew down empty streets. They flew over an overpass. She extinguished the red and blue lights, drove six blocks, and yanked the car into a U-Haul rental business. She nestled the car beside a box truck, facing Woodland Park Drive.

"Pray he has a car hauler at his house," said CJ as she threw a thumb over her shoulder. "Get the long gun and the extra clips while we have a chance."

Maria returned with an AR-15. "Ramirez is responsible for Sloan's death?"

With her mind on overdrive, CJ turned to Maria. "Everything points to his involvement. That includes Sloan's murder, making plastic keys on the duplicating machine and leaking inside information to Gloria Fishbaum."

Maria spoke volumes with her cold stare into the night.

Something bothering CJ bubbled to the surface. She searched her cell phone for a number and punched a name. A sleepy voice answered on the sixth ring.

"Sorry to bother you so late, but this is CJ and it's important."

She heard Randy yawn. "No problem."

"You borrowed Bob's Chevelle to go to work. Did a university cop stop you?"

"Not exactly. He pulled behind me and asked if he could look at her."

"Did he take your keys?"

"Yeah. He said he wanted to check on the restoration of the trunk and asked to borrow them. How did you know?"

CJ looked at Maria and nodded. Her attention turned back to Randy. "I owe you a steak dinner and a big apology. Go back to sleep."

"Huh?"

"I'll explain later."

Headlights of a vehicle cutting through the darkness brought CJ's full attention to the road in front of her. She relaxed as a Prius passed by.

Maria added another piece to the puzzle. "Sergeant

Ramirez is pretty lax with the officers except when it comes to their patrol assignments. He won't let them out of their area without permission."

"That fits. We don't know how the Mexican Mafia got to him. It's possible they selected him a long time ago. It's not unheard of that gangs and cartels are infiltrating police departments. Ramirez selected the cars and made sure no one with a badge was nearby when they smashed a window and hot-wired the car. Over time he discovered he could take pictures of keys during traffic stops and have duplicates made."

"What about the two druggies who took the Dodge truck on the day of Sloan's funeral?"

"They weren't Mexican Mafia, only locals cutting in on his business."

Maria seemed to digest the information. Her head tilted. "How did Sloan fit into the picture?"

A late model pickup pulling a trailer passed them. A delivery van followed close behind, both hastening toward the interstate. Maria pointed at the pickup. "That's Ramirez. He bought a dually a few days ago. It's used, but like new."

CJ waited for the vehicles to get a block ahead of them before she pulled out. With the delivery van blocking their view of Ramirez, CJ floored the accelerator. They gained ground fast. Maria leaned to her right. "His blinker's on. He's getting on the access road."

"The delivery van isn't turning." CJ pointed to a switch. "Get ready to deploy the Starchase."

Maria put her finger on the dash-mounted switch. CJ slid her car into the turn lane, nuzzling close to the trailer. The red beam of a laser shone on the trailer's tailgate. The 350 Dodge Ram diesel accelerated in a cough of black smoke and heart thumping noise.

"Now!"

The roar of the pickup's engine covered the sound of the Starchase being deployed. The tracker followed the red beam and stuck to the trailer's tailgate. CJ braked, pulled into an all-night convenience store, and watched the taillights of the truck speed toward the interstate.

After her heartbeat slowed, CJ pulled out her cell phone and punched in a speed dial for the ACU Police Department. "Rosemary, this is CJ. I've deployed Starchase. Begin tracking but stay off the radio with reports. Tell Lieutenant Grimes what's going on. Only communicate with me or Maria by this phone number or Maria's cell phone. Do you understand?"

"No radio to or from you. Got it."

"Chief Sylvester is on his way. Have him call me when he arrives. Maria and I will be southbound on I-35. Call if the tracker leaves the interstate."

CJ pulled her car back onto the access road and then onto the interstate. The fox and hound game of tracking Sergeant Ramirez began. She sped up until his taillights came into view and then backed off. Austin lay almost two hours away and Ramirez drove at a steady pace.

"This next call will be fun," said CJ. She punched in a number.

"I'M BUSY," SAID CAPTAIN CROW.

"I am too," said CJ. "We're both awake and have been most of the night."

"Are you calling to complain about missing the party in Austin?"

"You're not even close. I'm calling to tell you I've deployed a Starchase tracker on the tailgate of a car hauler driven by the man who's behind all the stolen cars at ACU. It isn't Speedy. It's one of my men, Sergeant Ramirez. My dispatch is tracking him and I'm a mile behind him, going south on I-35."

Captain Crow didn't respond for several seconds. "Call for backup and pull him over."

"That's not how I'm going to play this. David and I think there's a second chop shop. Ramirez is bound to have heard about the raid in Austin. I'll lay you ten-to-one odds he'll lead me to something interesting farther south."

"I... I don't know, CJ. You should take him down now."

"I have a question. Was that chop shop in Austin capable of stripping all the cars and trucks that are being stolen from the north and south areas?"

"The warehouse is big, but not that big. You may be right. He could lead us to a second shop."

"It won't hurt to find out."

"I'm afraid you're getting in over your head."

She gripped the steering wheel and ground her teeth. "Look. I'm not asking your permission. I'm keeping you informed of my activities as a courtesy. My best officer is with me with a loaded AR between her legs. We're going to find out where my crooked sergeant is going, with or without your help. Someone ordered a hit on one of my officers and I'm betting Ramirez is involved. I'm putting an end to this once and for all. Call me back if you're interested in catching some more bad guys."

CJ sensed Maria's gaze before she heard, "That... was... AWESOME!"

CHAPTER THIRTY-EIGHT

Traffic amounted to truckers trying to get to, through or around Austin before the city came to life. They approached the outskirts of Georgetown, twenty-odd miles north of the state capital. Maria's phone rang, and she put it on speaker. "It's dispatch."

"This is John. Suspect vehicle turned onto 130 Bypass. They're going around Austin."

In the distance, the pickup dropped down the far side of a rainbow-shaped overpass. CJ followed it onto a divided highway with a posted speed limit of 80 mph. Her cell phone came to life again.

"CJ, this is Clint. Whatever you said to Captain Crow put some chili powder in his shorts. He told me to get with you and give you anything you need."

"Good morning. Is David with you?"

"Right here. Are you stirring up trouble again?"

"Afraid so. Maria and I are tracking Sergeant Ramirez. He's hauling a stolen car from the university. We're heading south on Toll 130, going around Austin. I'm convinced he'll lead us to a second warehouse."

"He hasn't spotted you?" asked David.

"Starchase is wonderful. John's tracking and calling with updates."

"What do you need?" asked Clint.

"State troopers. But not too close."

"Will do. I'll see if the chopper is available to make sure they don't stick that fancy Starchase on a cattle truck."

CJ swerved to miss an armadillo. "One more thing. Ramirez has scanners in his truck. Maria and I are using cell phones."

As the miles passed CJ noticed a stream of headlights form a line about half a mile behind her. She maintained a constant speed and passed the major highway leading to downtown Austin. Onward they pressed, past the cut-off to Austin's airports.

A few minutes later, her phone rang. David's voice sounded like sandpaper. "We're still trying to get the chopper."

CJ spoke over him. "I'm approaching the intersection that either continues south or cuts west and joins back into I-35. I'll call you back."

Maria giggled. "He didn't sound happy."

The first glimmer of day broke over her left shoulder. CJ followed the four-lane divided highway south and chewed up miles. Once she passed Lockhart she said, "This road joins I-10, the main road between Houston and San Antonio. I'm betting he's not going much farther before he stops."

Maria wasn't one to gab, but they'd been traveling for almost three hours. "You never told me about Sloan."

"Oh, yeah," said CJ. "It's no secret Sloan hated me and David." She went on to explain that David was her trainer when she completed the highway patrol academy. Yari was her next-door neighbor at an apartment in Waco. "One of Yari's sorry boyfriends beat the stuffing out of her. I heard the racket through the paper-thin walls and kicked in her door. I cuffed the guy and David showed up without me calling him. Sloan responded for Waco PD and offered to transport the boyfriend to jail. He took the long way and gave the guy a serious attitude adjustment. A hot-shot lawyer caught wind of it and raised a stink. Sloan asked us to lie about what he'd done."

"Ah," said Maria.

"The department allowed Sloan to resign before they fired him. After that, he hired on at ACU. The civil suit bankrupted him. That was the last straw for Sloan's wife. She served him with divorce papers. He never caught up financially."

"He blamed you and David for his screw-up?"

CJ nodded. "Ramirez must have found out about what happened in Waco and saw it as a way to get a hook into Sloan. All he had to do was make a traffic stop and take a photo of a key. Easy money and little risk."

"So why was Sloan murdered?" asked Maria.

CJ checked the rearview mirror. The troopers trailed well behind her. "Believe it or not, I think Sloan grew a conscience. He hated me, but he also didn't enjoy being a dirty cop. He thought he could start over with Riverview PD. That's not the way gangs play. They didn't count on Sloan getting off a shot."

"How much of that can you prove?" asked Maria.

CJ raised her shoulders and let them fall. "Not much. At least not yet. The raid in Austin and the searches in Riverview should produce some answers. Who knows? Ramirez may be talkative once we get him in custody."

Maria patted the stock of the rifle. "Or he may do something stupid."

CHAPTER THIRTY-NINE

amirez's truck merged onto I-10, heading west toward
Seguin and San Antonio. CJ's phone rang again. Clint's
name appeared on the caller I.D.

"Captain Crow doesn't want this mess in a major popula-
tion area. I'm ordering spike strips halfway between Seguin
and San Antonio."

A huff of exasperation came out. "All right. That's the safe
thing to do. Where are you?"

"Waiting for the pilot. Troopers will close in on you when
you're three miles from the spike strips."

"Sounds good."

Before Seguin appeared in her rearview mirror, CJ closed
the gap on Ramirez. Maria said, "He's getting off the interstate. I can see his blinker."

CJ made the call to Clint. "Hold everyone back. He's
getting off the interstate. Let's see where he goes."

Maria's phone rang. She issued a series of "Okays," and
hung up. "The chief said there's no road showing where the
Starchase is. It must be a private drive."

A cloud of white dust rose from a gravel road. A sign

marked the way to Texas' Best Trailer Service. CJ said, "This is a perfect place to set up a chop shop. Who would suspect a trailer repair business?"

Dust billowed behind Ramirez's truck and trailer. Focused on the cloud, CJ didn't see the jeep pull out from behind a clump of Mesquite trees until it appeared in her mirror. The driver held a pistol in his left hand while the man riding shotgun had just that, a shotgun. She punched the accelerator and shouted. "Get on the phone to Blake. Tell them they spotted us and—"

The back glass exploded.

Maria shouted into her phone, "Shots fired! We're taking fire!"

The police interceptor engine kicked in. The car fishtailed but caught its grip and the jeep disappeared. Dust in front of her cleared as Ramirez turned left onto an asphalt driveway. He'd led them to the rear of a massive metal building and a large parking lot strewn with trailers of various sizes, shapes and states of disrepair.

"One way in, one way out," said CJ with nowhere to go but to follow Ramirez. She shot past an opened-mouthed Ramirez, who drew his pistol and fired a hurried shot.

CJ drove until she could drive no further and spun the wheel. The back end almost clipped the shell of a rusty horse trailer. CJ crouched behind the open driver's door and unloaded her .40 caliber Glock at Ramirez's truck as Maria squeezed off volleys from the rifle. Sergeant Ramirez's truck wasn't going anywhere but he'd already sprinted for the shelter of the building.

Empty clips rattled on the asphalt as both women reloaded.

Glancing back at the dirt road, the jeep that was following them came to a stop at the entrance of the parking lot, blocking them in.

Rapid but inaccurate shots came their way from inside the building and from the jeep that stopped where gravel met asphalt.

CJ crammed in another clip. "We're going to shoot and scoot. I'll provide covering fire and you run. Don't stop at the low-boy. Get behind that church van. When you get there, cut loose and I'll join you." She raised her pistol and squeezed off more rounds, tattooing the building's door. A lull occurred. CJ took off at a sprint as Maria's rifle riddled the shop with even more holes. Maria crammed a fresh clip home and continued to look down the sights of the rifle. "What now?"

"Let's see what they do. We may need to move again."

Sirens drew closer. It sounded like half the police in the state were converging on their location. CJ looked in the distance. A steady stream of state troopers and Sheriff's office vehicles rushed toward her location from San Antonio. A flash came from the middle door of the building. She heard a "whoosh." An explosion pierced the morning air and CJ found herself on the ground with ears ringing.

Maria hollered something in Spanish followed by, "What was that?"

"Rocket-propelled grenade."

Engulfed in flames, CJ's SUV crackled with the sounds of burning plastic, upholstery and gasoline. Pushed their direction by a southwest wind, the duo became engulfed in black acrid smoke.

"I think we may need to scoot some more," said Maria before she coughed. Taking advantage of the smoke, they duck-walked to the lee side of an abused bobtail truck and took up positions that afforded them a view of the metal building.

CJ coughed and took in a clean breath of air. "At least we can see from here and aren't being choked."

The first six highway patrol units arrived and blocked the dirt road with their cars and SUV's. The two men in the jeep abandoned their vehicle, choosing to run in the face of overwhelming odds. Additional state troopers came in quick succession while a helicopter circled high overhead.

CJ's phone rang. She punched it and heard David's strained voice. "Talk to me. Anyone wounded?"

"Not yet. But I'm not crazy about being shot at with RPGs. Think you might do something?"

"We're working on it. You have the right flank. Take cover and hold tight. Help is on the way."

Maria spoke while keeping her gaze locked on the front site of her rifle. "How far away from the building would you say we are?"

CJ glanced around the corner of the trailer. "A little over a hundred yards." She watched as a series of roll up doors came down. "Fix your aim on that small door in the middle. That's the only one they can exit without making a lot of noise."

Minutes passed and the rush of adrenaline waned. Maria remained fixed on the door while CJ monitored the right side of the building. She looked around at the unfamiliar setting. This was a long way from the campus of Agape Christian University, but this is where the trail had led her and this is where Ramirez would come to the end of his dual careers in law enforcement and as a car thief.

She heard, then felt, the blasts of rotor wash from a helicopter landing behind their position. Five heavily armed men exited into what looked like a Hollywood-created cloud of black smoke. Crouching low, they zig-zagged their way across open ground, cut a barbed wire fence and headed toward them. One fanned out past her burning car and sought cover in the bed of the low-boy trailer. Three more took up staggered positions to her left. One came straight for her.

"Who are they?" asked Maria, her gaze looking at what appeared to be a military unit.

"Ranger SWAT team," said CJ.

A helmeted ranger issued a terse, "CJ, looks like you have yourself a little situation here."

"Frank? Is that you under all that face paint and helmet?"

"We were on standby last night. Captain Crow wouldn't let us stand down. He told us you'd get into something this morning." He looked at Maria. "What's the status?"

"Are you talking to me?" asked Maria.

"Yes, ma'am. You have eyes-on."

"All garage doors are down, eight in total. One regular door in the center. We exchanged gunfire with the men inside. I counted nine men before the doors went down. Unknown if any civilians or hostages are inside. So far, we've received fire from a shotgun, semi-automatic handguns, and an RPG."

"No automatic weapons fire?"

"Not yet, but if that door cracks open, I won't wait to find out."

The ranger turned to CJ. "I like her."

"I like her, too. Why don't you take her place?"

"I'm fine where I am," snapped Maria. "I have a full clip and a clean shot at the door."

"How about a drink of water?" asked Frank.

"I'll take it."

He sidled beside Maria and tugged the mouthpiece of his Camelback loose. Extending the black hose to her mouth, she gulped down a few swallows and nodded.

Turning to CJ, Frank put a hand over the side of his helmet with a black cord snaking to an ear bud. "It's David. He wants you to go through the smoke to the crest of the hill behind us. Says he needs a spotter."

"What about Maria?"

"She's my protection." Frank smiled, but only for a second. "Get going, CJ."

One of the burning tires on her Tahoe exploded as she ran through the gap in the barbed wire. Another rush of adrenaline hit her and she scurried up the hill in the same zig-zag pattern the SWAT team had used to approach her. David had concealed himself so thoroughly on the hill's crest she almost stepped on him.

He didn't glance up but said, "Get on the spotter's scope and tell me if you can see any activity inside."

With deliberate movements, she set up the scope and focused on the center door. "Do we need to calculate distance, wind and elevation?" she asked.

"I'm already dialed in." He kept looking through the scope mounted to his 308. "Good to see you in one piece. When I heard that RPG round go off, I thought I might be a widower."

"Not today."

The roll-up door on the extreme right jolted upward, but only two feet. "Shift right," she said.

David swung the barrel of the rifle. CJ looked up to see the smaller middle door open and another flash. The second round from the RPG went straight for Maria and Frank, but sailed over their heads. She reached for David and buried her nose in the chalky dirt. Another explosion. Dust and rocks showered down on them.

Gunfire erupted from the team, all aimed at the open middle door.

"That was a cleaver diversion," said David in an even tone.

CJ focused her scope. "They have a large piece of sheet-metal that's acting like armor. The rounds are bouncing off. I can see a small opening that the RPG can fire through. If they get another round off, they're going to take out Maria and Frank."

The middle door remained open with a sheet of steel stopping small arms fire. David spoke to someone on the radio. She couldn't tell who. "You don't understand. If I don't take the shot, we'll have two dead officers."

He listened again, jerked the earpiece out and shook his head. "Idiots! Trying to manage a battle from a hundred miles away."

His gaze shifted to CJ. "The director doesn't want me to use the Barrett 50 cal. He's afraid of the publicity for using such a big caliber."

CJ looked at the rifle case behind David. She scooted down the hill, took it out of its case and loaded the clip containing the massive shells. "I don't answer to your director," said CJ.

David didn't hesitate. He moved to the spotter's scope and made way for CJ to take his place.

The butt of the rifle rested flat on her cheek as she pulled it tight against her shoulder.

"Watch your breathing," whispered David. "Two full breaths and relax... good... take in another and let it out halfway and squeeze. You should never know when the shot—"

CJ's shoulder absorbed the recoil as the round flew for less than half a second before it slammed into and through the metal shield. A second explosion rocked the area, but this time it came from inside the building.

"What happened?" asked CJ.

"Either the round blew the barrier back into whoever was firing the RPG, or it went through the barrier and took him out. Either way, their grenade went straight up. Everyone in there is stunned. Now's the time to hit hard."

The SWAT team and troopers sprinted to the building and entered. No more shots, only loud commands drifted up the hill on the smoke and the wind.

Minutes passed with David remaining motionless, looking through the spotter's scope.

CJ's gaze shifted to her husband. She tucked her feet under her like a coiled cat and pushed the rifle well in front of her. "Are you thinking what I'm thinking?"

He returned the same question.

She answered by launching herself on him and didn't rise until she had as much face paint on her as he did.

CHAPTER FORTY

CJ sipped her morning coffee. With the report on the raid filed in a mysterious storeroom called the cloud, she smiled with satisfaction. For the first time in what seemed forever, she fixed her mind on Christmas and all the things that remained undone.

Shuffling feet in the hall of the police department brought her back to the present. They grew louder and Yari poked her head in the door's opening.

"Got a minute?"

After waving her in she said, "I hear you're out on bond."

Yari's hair, a fading shade of green, bounced as her head nodded. "Aunt Bea paid my bail. I've been staying with her and Mr. Billy Paul."

"That's not permanent, is it?"

"I'll move on campus as soon as the dorms open for the spring semester. President Cummings said that's the only way I can keep my job. That and go to counseling."

CJ pointed to a chair. "Take a seat and relax."

"Yes, ma'am."

When had Yari last used that phrase? A few nights in jail must have left an impression on the wayward chef.

"What final agreement did you and the D.A. come to?" asked CJ.

"Three years' probation for my part in stealing a car. He dropped all other charges because I spilled my guts and I'll testify when the time comes."

"Speedy may be the only one you'll testify against. If he pleads guilty, you won't have to go to court at all."

Yari's head tilted. "Why not Sergeant Ramirez?"

"You didn't know it was him coordinating everything. What could you say?" CJ took a sip of coffee. "Besides, he sealed his fate when he shot at me and Maria. That's attempted capital murder. Then he grabbed the heavy artillery and blew up my SUV. That's all kinds of stupid. If he ever gets out of the state pen, he's looking at federal time."

"Is he still in the hospital?" asked Yari.

"David said they're still picking shrapnel out of him. They'll transfer him back to our county jail when he's well enough to travel."

CJ leaned forward. "You didn't come to pass the time of day. What's on your mind?"

Yari hung her head.

CJ circled her desk, pulled a chair close and sat almost knee to knee. "Tell me," she whispered.

Yari raised her quivering chin. "I don't get it. I'm such a doofus. I caused so much trouble and now everyone is helping me." She paused and locked her gaze on CJ. "Why?"

"You're a talented, hardworking and likeable woman." She patted Yari's knee. "But you pick lousy men."

Yari rolled her eyes and spoke with unbridled sarcasm, "Tell me about it. I've always been a bum-magnet."

"You don't have to be."

"That's what Aunt Bea and President Cummings say."

CJ cocked her head and said, "And?"

"Aunt Bea's on the lookout for a honeybee partner. President Cumming has me set up with a counselor."

"How does becoming a honeybee strike you?" asked CJ.

"A lot better than being a punching bag." Her eyebrows knitted together. "I never had a best friend. If I had one, I wouldn't have to settle for a hairy-legged scum bag."

CJ couldn't restrain her laugh. "You have a way with words."

Yari rose. "I came by to say thank you. You saved my life. Can I get a hug?"

"Any time you need one, come by."

The hands on the wall clock told CJ she couldn't tarry. One more stop and she could enjoy Christmas. Winter's cold fingers grabbed at her ankles as soon as she stepped outside.

THE WINTER GRADUATION CEREMONY AND SUBSEQUENT exodus had left the campus cold and empty. The only thing left on CJ's calendar was to attend the last board of regents meeting with John and Maria. Rumors circulated about a commendation of some sort. CJ walked across the quiet campus and imagined the scowling face of Gloria Fishbaum.

Maria stood at the base of the steps of the Administration Building, shivering and hugging herself.

"Why didn't you wait for me inside?" asked CJ.

Maria tilted her head toward the steps. "The lobby's full of reporters."

"Reporters? Why?"

Her shoulders rose and fell. "John seemed to know about it and Dotty's running the show."

Four news crews spilled out the door and began filming CJ and Maria as they ascended the steps.

CJ spoke to Maria through a clenched-teeth smile. "Don't say a word. Keep walking until we get to President Cummings' office."

Dotty met them at the top of the stairs and announced, "I'm sorry guys, but I need to get our heroes upstairs. You'll have quotes from them before you leave. I promise."

Something caught the reporters' attention. In unison, they cast their gazes to the street as a caravan of vehicles approached. Interest in CJ and Maria dropped like an anvil in a lake. A pair of highway patrol SUVs led the way with emergency lights activated. They escorted a black Suburban followed by two more black road-barges with windows tinted dark as pitch.

"What's going on?" asked Maria.

"Get upstairs fast," said CJ. "That's Governor Wainwright."

Maria stood frozen in place. "Who's that with him?"

CJ squinted and spoke with deliberation. "Captain Crow. I don't know about the other man and woman."

CJ and Maria scurried to Alice's office and were waved into the inner sanctum by a smiling secretary. John motioned them to sit by him. He raised an index finger to his lips, the signal to stay quiet.

Ms. Fishbaum's voice cut the air in the room like a rusty sword. "If you think I'll modify my words because these two have joined the meeting, you can think again. Using military grade weapons on civilians by law enforcement must never happen again. This is not a third world country."

Without a pause she continued. "Besides pretending to be Hollywood action movie stars, these two, under Chief Sylvester's direct supervision, abandoned their duty and jurisdiction. It's unconscionable that our personnel traveled hundreds of miles from this campus. Their theatrics have placed this university in a precarious legal position. Mark my words, the lame excuse about the doctrine of hot pursuit can and will be challenged by those who were so violently assaulted.

"And speaking of challenges. I hope everyone received my latest email concerning the projected drop in enrollment this coming spring. This directly results from top leadership being preoccupied to the point of being irresponsible and ineffective. It's a tragedy that Alice Cummings has allowed her sordid personal life to take her eyes off her responsibilities."

CJ took in a deep breath and counted to ten. To her surprise, nobody spoke up. Blood rushed to her head and her fists formed into tight balls.

John's hand covered one of her fists and he repeated the signal for her to keep quiet.

The rant continued. Alice, John, and all the board members listened with blank expressions. CJ wondered if a spell had turned them to stone.

When CJ made eye contact with Billy Paul, he did something she'd never witnessed. He winked.

The door to Alice's office flew open. In blew Governor Charlie Wainwright, complete with entourage in his wake. He wasn't a tall man, but his shoulders spread wide. His set countenance reflected that of a man on a mission.

He opened with, "I'll save the pleasantries until after we take care of business." His gaze shifted to the woman intent on seeing CJ, John, Alice and Maria fired. "Ms. Fishbaum, I'd like to introduce you to Captain Crow of the Texas Rangers. Beside him are Special Agents Harrison and Summerfield of the FBI. Agents from Homeland Security and ATF wanted to join us but I told them they could entertain the reporters gathered downstairs."

He turned to the man wearing a blue suit. "Agent Harrison, she's all yours."

The agent moved to a spot in front of the attorney, while the other federal agent circled behind her. "Gloria Fishbaum, you're under arrest. Put your hands behind your back."

The verbal barrage began and didn't wane until the agents and Captain Crow hustled her out of the room.

John leaned toward CJ. "Perp walk with every major network here to record it for the evening news. Dotty set it up."

CJ noticed Maria covered her mouth to keep from smiling.

The atmosphere of the room changed from unpleasant business to happy hour. Alice's secretary wheeled in a cart with champagne and other adult beverages. Yari pushed a second cart loaded with decadent treats. Governor Wainwright started with Alice and worked his way around the table to shake hands and slap backs.

CJ used the noise to cover her grilling of John. "Why am I the only one in the dark?"

"It's simple. Gloria owns the law firm that defends the Mexican Mafia. It's a shadow firm under another attorney's name, but the money's traced to her."

CJ's mouth flew open.

John continued. "David noticed how fast many of those involved in the two raids made bail. He grilled Ramirez until he broke. Ms. Fishbaum didn't stop with defending the gang members. Ramirez knew enough to get the Feds interested in her involvement in obtaining the RPGs and mortars and other military toys the raids produced. She's looking at serious time under RICO charges."

"Why didn't David tell me?"

"He wanted her arrest to be your Christmas present."

CJ stood and looked out a window. Halfway down the

sidewalk, Gloria Fishbaum turned from the swarm of reporters. She cast her gaze at Alice's office window and took a last look at a place where she would never be welcome again. CJ raised her right hand with her palm toward the window. With only her fingers she waved and whispered, "Checkmate."

Thanks for reading *A Murder Redeemed*. I hope it satisfied your appetite for a good mystery and kept you turning the pages to find out 'whodunit.' I would be very grateful if you would take a minute to leave a review at your favorite retail site, Bookbub or Goodreads. Reviews are the lifeblood of books and you, the reader, can keep that lifeblood flowing!

I'd love for you to join my mystery lovers community. You'll be among the first to know about new releases, discounts and recommendations. After you sign up you'll receive the first perk of being a Mystery Insider, a free David and CJ short story!

You can also follow me on Amazon, Bookbub and Goodreads to receive notification of my latest release.

Thanks again for reading!
Bruce

Scan above or go to bit.ly/Back-Road-Justice.

Drawing from his extensive background in criminal justice, Bruce Hammack writes contemporary, clean read detective and crime mysteries. He is the author of the Smiley and McBlythe Mystery series, the Fen Maguire Mystery series and the Star of Justice series. Having lived in eighteen cities around the world, he now lives in the Texas hill country with his wife of thirty-plus years.

Follow Bruce on Bookbub and Goodreads for the latest new release info and recommendations. Learn more at brucehammack.com.